HEIR OF RUIN

FAE OF THE SAINTLANDS: BOOK ONE

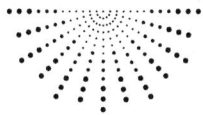

LEIGH KELSEY

Fae of the Saintlands is RH, which means Maia doesn't have to choose between her many lovers. This series contains mature scenes intended for adult readers.

This book was written, produced, and edited in the UK where some spelling, grammar and word usage will vary from US English.

Copyright © Leigh Kelsey 2021

All rights reserved. No part of this publication may be reproduced or transmitted in any form or by any means, electronic or mechanical, without the prior written permission of the author

The right of Leigh Kelsey to be identified as author of this work has been asserted by her in accordance with the Copyright, Designs and Patents Act 1988

www.leighkelsey.co.uk

Want an email when new books release - and four freebies?
Join here by clicking here

Or chat with me in my Facebook group: Leigh Kelsey's Paranormal Den

Cover by https://fantasybookdesign.com/

❦ Created with Vellum

BLURB

A brand new reverse harem fae romance series inspired by Hades and Persephone that fans of Truthwitch and Throne of Glass will devour.

A princess with untold power...

Maia Delakore is the tool of her aunt, the queen of the Vassal Empire. With her snaresong magic, Maia moulds the minds of the court, and eradicates any resistance to the queen's reign. But when her aunt commands her to kill a prince, she refuses. And flees into the arms of the crown's worst enemy —the Sapphire Knight.

A fae lord with a secret...

Azrail and his sister are all that's left of a family framed for treason. As the Sapphire Knight, he and a small band of friends wreak havoc on the queen's plans, sparing those sentenced to death, and sneaking the hunted beastkind— humans with an animal form—out of the city. But when they save a young girl with a rare, powerful magic, Azrail and his friends are drawn into a plot laid by the saints themselves.

A plot that will draw Azrail and Maia together, sparking a love that will become legend.

Fantasy romance readers will adore this fated mates, enemies to lovers series, with a kickass princess, a snarky fae lord, a seductive prince, and a sweet male courtesan. Sizzling romance meets dangerous magic in this epic, sweeping story of fate and darkness.

This book is slow burn, but hot in later books, and has multiple love interests added throughout the series. 50,000 words.

For the Reverse Harem Readers and Authors Facebook group.

This book is all your fault.

NOTE

The Saintlands series is slow burn romance with multiple love interests. The romance will develop over the series, but I *promise* it'll be worth the wait—and steamy enough to melt your kindle from book two.

I hope you love Azrail, Kheir, and Jaro!

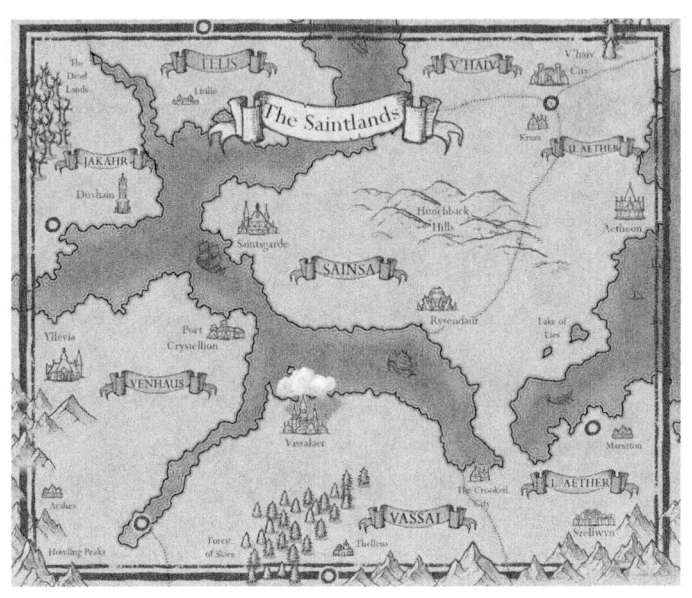

CHAPTER ONE

The Delakore family pennant flapped violently in the breeze off the Luvasa River as Azrail slipped through the crowd. His sister and their two friends wove through the gathering at equal points of the compass, all of them converging, in secret, around the guillotine set up in the center of the Salt King's Square. It was a rare overcast day in Vassalaer, the City of Skies covered with dark clouds that threatened to ruin the jubilation and spectacle, and the scent of a storm clung to Az's nostrils as he took a calming breath.

Days like these made Azrail sick, and not just because his innocent parents had been hung as traitors in this square while onlookers exactly like those around him watched with wide mouths and delightfully scandalised gasps. It was the hunger that made him nauseated, the eagerness of the crowd as they clamoured forward with greedy eyes, hungry for any glimpse of the green-clad hangman or the criminal whose life was about to be cut short. People even hung out of the windows of bright coloured houses that lined the river, eager for the spectacle.

Half the criminals executed here had committed minor crimes. A lot of them weren't even guilty. Some rare criminals, Az could admit, were worthy of the sentence, but *all* of them? If every executed person was guilty, then Azrail was a welcomed, upstanding member of court.

He snorted softly at the idea. He and his sister had been forgotten at best and reviled at worst since their parents' executions when he was sixteen and Evrille was a baby. They'd only managed to live because their parents had caused a big enough magical distraction for Az to flee with his baby sister when they were arrested.

The crowd jeered, and Azrail honed his attention on the wooden platform built several feet above them—so everyone would be afforded a clear view of the killing. And today's killing... it was bad. Worse than bad. Unforgivable.

Az and his band of secret insurgents had received a short message last night from a guard ally in the palace, just six words long.

Execution. Tomorrow. She's eight years old.

It had been enough for Az, his sister Evrille, and their two friends Zamanya and Jaromir to begin planning immediately, staying up all night as they hammered their plan into shape, smoothing out the cracks and holes until they had something that could work.

It *would* work. If it didn't, a girl would be killed. A girl who, like her late mother, was accused of being a traitor, and who was completely undeserving of murder. There was no justifiable reason the crown would condemn an eight-year-old to death.

Grey sunlight glinted off a pocket watch to Azrail's right, a completely ordinary occurrence but one he'd been watching for. Jaromir was in place. Az adjusted his costume glasses until a flash of watery light bounced off them, waiting for Zamanya's and Evrille's signals. The flashes came quickly;

they were all ready. And as the hangman shoved the sobbing girl towards the wooden block on the stage, stained dark after years of executions, Az sent his awareness tunnelling down into the earth, threads of subtle green magic streaming from his fingers.

The stones beneath his feet reached up to him, the dirt far below them shivering with eagerness, and the big oak trees planted on the edges of the riverside square rustled their leaves and pulsed with old, old power. Power Azrail had always been able to access as one of Vassalaer's five hundred fae residents. He wasn't as powerful as some of the long-lived fae, nor as knowledgeable as those who'd studied at the universities in Sainsa Empire, but he had a natural ability he'd always been able to draw upon, and he yanked on it now, asking the earth to aid him.

The stones responded first, shuddering beneath his feet. Ripples went through the crowd, a call of alarm. Their last earthquake had caved in the Allsaints Temple, reducing it to ruins, so the people were rightly wary. Not that Azrail would let this quake destroy any buildings—just the people responsible for sentencing an eight-year-old girl to death. The same people who'd sentenced his parents to death.

The girl stood on the stage, staring with wide eyes as the hangman paused, her pale lilac dress dirty with grime and her fair hair in a ratty ponytail, her face as smeared with dirt as the rest of her.

But as Az moved through the crowd, pulling a mask of panic over his predatory concentration, the girl's eyes caught his gaze: bright and shining, a lone spot of colour in a sea of grey features. They were a rare violet, so deep and vibrant that he'd never seen eyes like it before. And they were full of terror—and defiance. She had spark, and Az smiled just as the girl threw her elbow into the hangman's gut and fled for the edge of the platform. The need for revenge pounded in his blood, a roar between his ears, a constant need to make those who'd killed his parents pay—and he recognised the same vengeance and defiance in the girl.

Those closest to her screamed in fright, and one word spread through the crowd, making Az's pursuit falter.

Saintslight...

That was impossible. No one had wielded saintslight in a hundred years, not since the last Ghathanian Queen had been murdered in her sleep, a Delekore rival taking her place. *That* queen was said to have been blessed by the saints themselves, and able to commune with them, to draw on their purest light to heal ... and to destroy.

Their guard ally hadn't mentioned what magic the girl had, or even what her crimes were, but this...

The guards must not have known. No way in the Wolven Lord's dark chasm would the queen and crown let a girl with saintslight be executed in public. No, they'd keep that private to stop word spreading to other empires—empires that might shelter and revere the girl instead of despise and fear her.

Azrail pocketed his costume glasses and abandoned all pretense of being a panicked onlooker, begging the cobbles to speed him across the square as he sprinted, a tightness cinching his chest. It couldn't be saintslight. It had to be a different fae magic that *looked* like saintslight. But the fear that infected the crowd was sharp and unwavering, the kind of fear that came from seeing, not just hearing rumours.

A flash came from his left, Evrille signalling something, but they had planned for this kind of chaos, and Azrail intended to take advantage of it. The executioner had recovered and now he dove for the girl just as she leapt off the wooden platform into the crowd with a cry. Az's heart stuttered, but he didn't stop running, the stones beneath his feet carrying him at a swift pace.

He aimed for a gap in the crowd, as if they'd all backed away to create a ring of emptiness around the girl, and this time he asked the dirt for help, sketching a streak of bright green power in the air with a quick gesture. His blood thrummed as a wall of earth and rocks shot up from the ground to push back the few men looking to confront the girl—or to subdue her so she could be executed as planned.

At the show of his earth magic, the girl spun, and a searching power slid along his own magic like the cold breath of moonlight. She scanned the crowd, and fixed her eyes on Azrail as he shoved through the last few people, holding out a deep gold hand.

"Come with me," he urged, breathless. The woman he'd pushed aside to reach the girl walloped him with her leather bag, and Az snorted, turning to pin the aging woman with a dark look as his ribs throbbed.

The woman squeaked, backing up at the warning she read in his face, and Az returned his gaze to the girl with fading amusement. "Fast now, or they're going to catch you."

"Hey!" someone shouted, a gravelly male voice. Not the executioner, but likely a concerned citizen who'd come here to see justice done, a traitor to the empire killed, and the city made safe. Safe from a little girl. Az didn't bother looking at the man; he just sent an image at the nearest tree and heard its roots creak and snap out. He didn't watch them snag around his ankle as the man yelled, "What do you think you're—*what the saints?*"

The girl's violet eyes jumped past Azrail, watching the man dangle in the air. It was effortless, a small enough magic that he didn't even feel a pull on his reserves. The girl laughed, her violet eyes crinkling and her dirty face splitting in a grin. That grin was as good as spitting in the face of the queen and crown. That grin was the reason Az risked his life to save people like her, why he never gave up.

"What's your name?" Azrail asked her, exhaling in relief as he spotted Zamanya breaking through the crowd in her dark burgundy leathers, snapping obscenities at onlookers' shocked faces and throwing fists into their ribs if they lingered too long for her liking. She'd been a warrior in the Vassalaer army once, and now she was general of Azrail's ranks, few and sparse though they were.

"Siofra," the girl replied, her expression guarded as she scanned the people watching, restless on her feet. Surrounded and caged; Az hated the feeling, too. "What's yours?"

"I'm Azrail," he replied so only she heard, keeping an eye on the people around them. "Come on, you look like you could use a bath."

Her eyes brightened, her whole demeanour changing. "With hot water?

"As hot as you can stand it," he promised, keeping his hand held out to her until she slipped her small palm into it. "See that big woman over there? That's my friend Zamanya. And just there, that woman in the brown leather jacket, that's my sister Evrille."

"The one who looks mean and angry?"

Az snorted. "Yeah, that one. And that man there, with the red ponytail, that's my best friend Jaromir. We're here to save you, Siofra."

Her eyes narrowed, her brows pushing together, crinkling her grimy face. "Why?"

The question shot into his heart like an arrow. So much confusion, as if she never considered that anyone might save *her*. What had she thought, locked in her cell awaiting execution? Had she had no hope of rescue, no one at all she'd dreamt would break her out? Az wanted to gather her into his arms, paternal instincts riding him hard.

"Have you heard of the Sapphire Knight?" he asked softly,

but apparently not softly enough, for the people who'd been pressing curiously around them gasped and shrank back, fleeing entirely. His mouth curved. His reputation really did precede him these days.

Siofra still watched him warily, but she nodded. "He blew up the palace gardens."

Az tried not to smile too smugly. That had screwed up a trade deal that would have brought more silk into the city and taken more indentured beastkind—humans with an animal form they could shift into at will—out of it.

"Well, you're looking at him." Az winked. "The Sapphire Knight, at your service." He swept a little bow, watching the crowd from the corner of his eye, his earth magic keeping them at bay so they couldn't make out his features—for now. "You'll be safer with me and my friends than on your own. And we've got a hot fire, as many baths as you desire, and a chicken roasting at home."

Her violet eyes went as wide as the moon. "Okay. Okay, I'm coming."

"For the baths or the chicken?" he asked, squeezing her hand. He created a path, shoving people aside with a wall of tree roots, leading Siofra through the square as his friends converged around them, a reassuring unit at his back.

"Both," Siofra replied, giving him a tentative smile.

"As *if*." Zamanya snorted at something beyond their sight. She flicked her dark hand, bright gold magic streaking through the air and sending the executioner soaring back onto his platform. He hit it hard enough to break bones, gold threads keeping him there.

"Woah," Siofra breathed, staring at the fae general in awe. "Can you teach *me* how to do that?"

Zamanya guffawed, scanning the crowd with both her eyes and tendrils of power, her powerful body on high alert. "In a few years, little hellion. In a few years."

"Aw," Jaromir laughed, batting long red hair from his face to give Siofra a conspiratorial look. "She's given you a nickname. I think that means she likes you."

Zamanya ignored him, sweeping her arm out and clearing them a wider path to the Luvasa where a boat waited for them, its red sails punching the sky.

"That was easy," Evrille remarked gruffly, coming up beside Az, her dark braid slapping her shoulder with every step and her green eyes blunt and irritated. But that was her usual expression, so Az wasn't sure if she was in a good mood or a bad one.

As if the saints had heard her remark, a resounding boom went through the Salt King's Square, shoving onlookers aside as a score of guards—Foxes in Delakore orange wielding magic-tipped spears—appeared from a plume of gold.

"Son of a bitch," Evrille growled.

"You really shouldn't tempt fate," Jaromir said, a wince on his elegant face. "Or swear—you know, children present."

"I *knew* I should have killed that executioner," Zamanya muttered, magic building around her in crackling gold. "He must have called for help."

"Either way," Az said, pulling Siofra closer as they all paused, searching for a way around the Foxes standing between them and the river. These bastards had taken enough people; he wouldn't let them touch a single hair on Siofra's head. "We're going to have to fight our way through that lot. Any ideas?"

"I've got one," Jaro said, tugging his hood closer over his face, no doubt spotting one of his clients in the group of soldiers marching towards them. "Run!"

"But the *boat*," Ev growled, throwing a glare at him. "Do you know how much it costs to rent that thing?"

"Not as much as our lives are worth," Az said firmly, grabbing Siofra and ignoring her bark of complaint as he picked her up, setting her on his hip. "We run. *Now*."

As much as he wanted to unleash himself and his magic on the Foxes, it was more of a *fuck you* to the crown if they escaped, if they lived. So, he gave the Foxes a sharp grin and ran.

CHAPTER TWO

Clouds chugged across the Vassalaer sky, their fluffy bottoms lit in shades of peach and rose as the sun began to set over the City of Skies. Maia watched the cloudy pastel sky through every tall window the royal procession passed, even though she should have been paying attention to her aunt Ismene, Queen of the Vassal empire. The view from this wing of the palace had always been her favourite: the pale spires, the low-slung mist and clouds, and the moonstone towers that thrust up to the sky, higher than every other building.

Maia arched her neck for a glimpse of her favourite building, a sprawling construction of arches, towers, and golden domes that contained more books than she could ever hope to read in a lifetime. This was the Library of Vennh, named for the Hunchback Saint—the patron of knowledge. Hopefully this meeting would be over quickly, and Maia could shove off the mantle of being the loyal princess of the Vassal Empire—and all the darkness that came with obeying the queen—and cross the city to her little attic room in the library. It had once been a study room for lords and ladies, its close proximity to the skies befitting their status, but Maia had filled it with secrets and theories.

"Daydreaming again, princess?" Lord Erren's silken voice asked, the captain of the royal guard's shadow falling over Maia's view of the city.

Her gaze went flat, the only outward sign of irritation she let show. She was an expert at this, at masking her real thoughts and opinions because they weren't *suitable* for polite society. Honestly, if Maia let her mask slip and allowed her aunt's people to see the coarse, foulmouthed woman she really was, they'd be scandalised.

A smile curled her mouth at the thought, but then Erren spoke again, and her gaze went even flatter.

"Don't let your aunt catch your mind drifting; you know how much she hates inattention." About as much as she hated untidiness. Maia eyed the three buttons undone on Erren's shirt, the balding spot in his corn silk hair, three sweaty hairs messily covering the area.

"I was paying perfect attention," Maia replied sweetly, giving the slimy royal adviser a placid smile. "I saw you and Lady Mindal exchange a touch just minutes ago. I'm so glad to see you happy, Lord Erren, you truly deserve all the good things that are coming to you."

Like a broken nose and a black eye when *Lord* Mindal found out.

Maia gave him an innocent smile full of so much sweetness it rotted her teeth, and increased her speed to catch up to her best friend, and the queen's lady in waiting, Naemi.

Naemi slid an amused glance at Maia, her golden hair pinned tightly with an owl comb and not budging even with the movement. Maia hid a smile, knowing exactly what Naemi would have to say about Erren.

Both forced to attend the same events, Naemi and Maia had been friends since childhood, when Maia had arrived from Saintsgarde in a political exchange between her mother, the queen of the Sainsa Empire, and her aunt. Her cousin Ilta had been raised in Saintsgarde, like Maia had been raised in Vassalaer, in a bid to continue the good relations between the empires and sister queens. Not that Maia's parents and her aunt actually got along; no, they *hated* each other, but to save face, they pretended to be a normal family.

The whole palace was made up of it: pretense.

Maia was no stranger to pretending herself, keeping her expression placid and her eyes carefully neutral as they reached a tall, sweeping staircase with bannisters capped by large, lifelike air drakes, the motif of the Eversky, saint of the skies. Sunlight gilded the lifelike veins in their wings, lovingly tracing their long, elegant necks and feathered wings. Maia had a favourite one, on the right bannister at the bottom. It was as big as a carriage and had a chip in its right ear, as if a rival drake had taken a bite out of it. Maia liked to imagine the drake was secretly a fighter, all elegant lines and beauty but a menace of teeth and claws lurking beneath, just like Maia.

Not that she had an animal form, like the beastkind the queen hated so much. It would be nice sometimes, though, to escape this skin and prowl through the woods as a panther, or soar the skies as a fearsome hawk.

Maia trailed her fingertips over the neck of the air drake as she passed it at the bottom of the stairs, and imagined she could feel its body expand with a breath. Anything to distract her from what came next. It was never good when she was asked to accompany her aunt and her retinue; it meant her aunt had a use for Maia's magic.

But Maia had been raised as a dutiful princess—and the consequences of disobeying were too painful and bloody—so no matter how much she hated the tasks she was given, she completed them. And got rip-roaring drunk afterward to blot out the memories of empty, staring eyes. And worse, the screams and hate-filled glares of those who fought back.

But it could have been worse; at least her skull wasn't stuck in a crystal box in the middle of the atrium for all to see and sneer at. The retinue of ladies and lords did just that as they passed the skull of the last Ghathanian Queen, a warning to anyone who thought to topple Ismene.

Maia secretly thought the crown were scared of the old queen's magic, even though it had died out two hundred years ago with the first Delakore Queen—saintslight, that divine magic of the saints themselves.

Maia wouldn't have minded having some saintslight herself; maybe she could use it to escape this hell.

"Maia," her aunt's clear voice rang through the hall as the retinue turned away from the high-ceilinged atrium into a low, cosy reception room. It was clearly meant for putting guests at ease with its informal setting. Curtains of rich Delakore orange framed tall windows, looking out on a silver curve in the Luvasa river and its many sunstone bridges, clouds drifting by beyond the glass. Plump soft furnishings invited the people who sat on them to relax, to let their guards down. And it worked. Grateful to not be paraded through a court of watchful eyes to stand before a high throne, the guests who entered this room were calm and easy targets.

The retinue parted, and Maia swiftly moved through lords and ladies and guards, pausing at her aunt's left side, a step behind, waiting for orders. For the axe to fall.

"We're meeting the V'haivan emissaries today; you're to stay close by us and be unremarkable as you do your job. This is your target for the next hour," she added, and neatly passed back a small square of cream paper, upon which a sketch had been drawn. Maia's target was an aging bronze-skinned man with dark hair threaded with grey, deep set eyes, and pouchy cheeks. A man his age would either succumb easily to her magic, or resist, long used to holding his own. And there'd be no way to tell which type he was until she'd already wrapped the invisible strands of her power around him.

Her mission was the same every time: get them to agree to whatever the queen wanted. The faces changed, the reasons shifted, but the outcome was always the same. Guests bent and surrendered, and Ismene Delakore, queen of the Vassal Empire, got her way. Maia was an unwilling tool of it all, but she didn't fancy adding more scars to her body, so she did as she was told.

Taking another glance at the portrait until she had a clear image in her mind, Maia crumpled up the paper and stuffed it into the pocket of her dress. Today she wore deep charcoal grey, with accents of orange—of course—and heavy beading all over. The fabric of her skirts shone like streaks of fire whenever it caught the light just so. It was her favourite dress to date, and she'd been planning to wear it to Silvan's music hall with Naemi tonight, but this job would ruin her love of it. It was always the same, the guilt-laced memory attaching itself to what she wore, or how she had her hair, or what strain of music was playing, or what she was eating at the time.

Shoving the dread far away, Maia sat on the sofa to the left of her aunt's high-backed chair as silver-clad men and women bustled into the room with a tea-cart, setting out smoky teaglasses—the only hint to Ismene's Sainsan heritage—on the short table before them. Maia took a drink just to calm her nerves, letting the warm infusion work its magic on her tense muscles. She shared a smile with Naemi as her friend sat beside her, reaching for a lightning biscuit and snapping it into two pieces along the bolt impressed in its surface in honour of the Eversky's immense magic. She passed Maia one half, and Maia mouthed, "Thank you," already feeling less stressed about this task with her friend beside her.

"They're approaching," Lord Erren announced, standing beside the queen with his back straight and strands of white magic twining between his fingers, ready to jump in front of the queen to defend her if the V'haivan emissaries decided to turn this meeting into an ambush. Some had tried over the years; they were all rotting in the bottom of the Luvasa.

"Let them stew for a minute outside," Ismene said, sipping her tea. She was the picture of composure, not a pale strand of hair out of place, not a wrinkle or frown line in her beautiful face. Icy—cold enough to burn. "It'll do them good."

Maia crunched the honeycomb biscuit, sweetness bursting across the tongue as well as a sharp, fizzing sensation that only the head cook of the palace could achieve, a creation of baking and magic. But the sweetness soured in her mouth when the queen nodded minutes later, and the retinue entered the room.

Two haughty lords, a handsome prince, a bored knight, and three eager merchants. All with wings on show, as was the V'haivan tradition. Maia couldn't imagine having that vulnerability exposed every moment of every day. Her wings —like most people's in the Vassal empire—were always, *always* hidden in a pocket of magic. But the wings of the emissaries caught the pale gold sunlight streaming through the bank of filigree windows, as sheer and beautiful as gossamer, varying in shades of sunset, ocean, and forest. The prince's were a rich copper membrane threaded with bright gold. Maia's were jade green and silver, not that she'd shown them to a single soul. Not even Naemi. It was taboo in the Vassal Empire—and a good way to signal weakness to your enemies. As part of the crown, Maia would have to be mad to show her wings.

Her target turned out to be a merchant, and a cloth one judging by the fine quality of his long tunic and the silk trousers he wore beneath. Maia watched him from the corner of her eye, beginning to hum a tune no one would hear but her, sending invisible strands of power across the expensive rug as he sat, deep into the merchant's mind. She didn't hear his name when the emissaries were introduced; it didn't matter. What mattered was that he was human, and had no magic of his own, and when Maia hummed louder, not letting her lips move, blending into the background so no one would notice her working magic, his mind gave way as easily as a knife through jelly.

Her stomach twisted into a knot at the sensation of tumbling into his head, but she ignored it, weaving a more intricate melody into her song. The merchant's brown pupils dilated, just slightly, and he was hers.

But when the queen spoke next, Maia wanted to turn her power on her aunt, twist *her* mind until she was screaming and howling and clawing at her skull. If Maia even tried, the palace guard would have her impaled with swords, spears, and magic within seconds. And a worse fate than death would be waiting for her after. She knew; she'd already lived it once.

"And what do you say, Sir Valleir?" Ismene asked, managing to be both regal and friendly, her pale head tilted and her brilliant blue eyes crinkled with an artful smile. "Are *you* opposed to expanding our trade caravans to include more merchandise?"

Such a normal word—merchandise. A word used to describe spices and cotton and books. And *people*. They traded in beastkind mostly, and lesser fae sometimes; those who wouldn't be missed. Those Maia was supposed to sneer at and despise. Except she never had. Her greatest secret was that she *hated* her aunt's laws, but she could never speak out about her beliefs. Maia had angered her once when she was thirteen, and she still bore the scars of her punishment.

It was easier, and *safer*, to be the dutiful, obedient princess in public, and to rage in secret. Even if condoning it—no, actively *encouraging* it—left a taint on her soul. Made a kernel of self-hatred form in her chest, in the heart of the wooded glade that Maia had always pictured her soul as.

Valleir blinked at Ismene's question, and then said, "I agree, both our empires could benefit from an increase in the caravans. But doubling the number could be too much too soon," he added, as Maia hummed, twisting his mind to and fro, moulding it until the thoughts she placed felt as natural as his own, his voice full of nothing but genuine feeling. "But a quarter increase this season would be easy enough, and then if that goes to plan, we can increase it again next season."

"We should be talking about *de*creasing the trade," the prince growled quietly, giving Sir Valleir a dirty look. Like all his people, Prince Kheir had deep gold skin, but instead of his companions' black locks, he had thick, wavy hair the colour of bronze. Passion shone from chocolate eyes, and with the dark stubble on his jaw, he was somewhere between rugged and elegant. A strange counter to the icy tones of Vassaler. And devilishly handsome—with morals to boot. It was a damn shame visitors were off limits for sleeping with, or Maia would happily tangle with the prince. "Not *in*creasing it," he went on, growing louder. "Dress it up however you want, you're trading in *people*."

Ismene's smile froze, and Maia's heart tripped. She didn't dare stop humming, keeping Sir Valleir in her thrall. It was an effort to keep her expression neutral, to keep her head still even as she wanted to nod and emphatically agree with the prince. He was the only person who'd spoken sense in this palace in weeks. The only person with a conscience it seemed.

But beastkind were nothing but animals to fae like her aunt. *Worse* than animals, sometimes.

"And harm the economies of both our empires?" Ismene asked the prince with a confused frown. Maia had known her aunt long enough to see the minutiae of anger in her unnaturally wrinkle-free face, but she hid it well. "This trade route kept our people fed and housed throughout the long siege of twenty-seven. To cut it, or *saints forbid*, end it altogether would remove a safety net we both need."

Prince Kheir's lush mouth thinned, but he didn't say anything else, sitting back in his seat and twisting a gold button on his embroidered sleeve around and around. Biding his time, probably, as Maia would have done. Ismene wasn't the sort of queen to be convinced of something on day one. Day three hundred and one, maybe. Maia sensed a long and painful negotiation ahead, and she could already feel the headache of manipulating it to her aunt's victory.

"Sir Gavan," Ismene said in a neutral tone, turning from the prince, her expression open and friendly once more. "What's your decree? For or against keeping our empires secure?"

Oh, clever. Instead of selling people into wars they would never come home from, they were safeguarding the people they actually cared about. It was rare in emissaries like this to find someone like the prince, whose morals outweighed his greed and selfishness. As long as their own families were unaffected, most people Maia met in this room were happy to sign anyone else's lives away.

Ironic that most people she met out in Vassalaer—commoners without a crown or title to their name—were more compassionate than the people in the palace, who held millions of lives in their grasp.

"I don't see a reason to decrease trade," Gavan replied, slicking white hair from his face. That was no surprise; he was a weaselly little man, and he and Ismene got along well. "Why not increase it?"

And that pretty much set the tone for the whole meeting. Maia was glad when it broke apart; she gave Naemi a squeeze on her shoulder and made her excuses to her aunt, who didn't show one sign of giving a shit as Maia slipped out of the door and walked—calmly, though she wanted to run—through the pale, gilded halls of the palace and up to her room.

Saints, she needed a drink. Naemi would be stuck with Ismene for another hour or so, but Maia knew her friend would meet her at the music hall. So Maia threw off the mantle of princess—a mental weight more than a physical one, and so much heavier for it—and added a dark line to her eyes, a rosy glow to her pale cheeks, and honeyed gloss to her lips, brushing out her hair until it shone like a sleek star. The dress was immaculate, so there was no need to change that, but she swapped her sensible shoes for a pair of strappy sandals and grabbed a glitzy bag she kept money and perfume in for these occasions.

Even though she'd stopped humming minutes ago, she could still feel the doughy sensation of Valleir's mind, could still sense the confusion that had filled his head in the split second before she took control and rearranged his wants, beliefs, and everything that made him *him*.

It's done. There's no going back, only forward.

Maia rolled her shoulders back, lifted her chin, and banished thoughts of snaresong, manipulation, and slave caravans as she headed for the palace's southern exit that led through the two-storey hedgerow and into Vassalaer proper.

She'd better make it two drinks.

CHAPTER THREE

Azrail held Siofra tighter to his side as the Foxes surged towards them, watery sunlight catching the brass buttons on their orange uniforms, the sharp edges on their spears and arrows shining like fire.

"Zamanya," Az bit out, whirling away from the Foxes, checking his sister and friends were following as he ran and not staying by the Luvasa to do something stupid and heroic. It wouldn't have been the first time. Or the eighth. "Zamanya!" he snarled again.

"Forsaken saints, Az, I know!" she snapped back. One glance at his friend showed her onyx arms slashed with golden magic, like sunlight through cracked bark. Streaks of burnished power gathered around her hands, strong enough to—with any luck—knock aside the Foxes who'd lurched after Az and his family as they sprinted away from that bloody square.

The bright colours of the riverside huts and houses blurred past as Az's feet pounded the paving stones, earth magic shuddering through him. His power reached out to every speck and mineral in the cobbles beneath him, ready to defend him when he gave the command.

Beneath the well of earth, a darker, more cunning magic cracked an eye open, warily watching as Az skated around a cart thick with the scent of fresh honey cakes and sugared saints. He stifled a wince at the stallholder's bark of complaint —and the frightened gasp that followed as she noticed the score of Foxes chasing them, the woman reassessing Azrail, Ev, Zamanya and Jaromir. From nuisances to dangerous criminals. Her brown eyes lit on Siofra held tight in Az's arms as he ran past, the girl eerily still and calm in his arms. Just as they ran out of sight of the sweets cart, the vendor's eyes narrowed with realisation that this girl was the one destined for the butcher's block. Fear paled her copper skin as she staggered back.

"It's alright," Az murmured as Siofra marked her reaction too, her violet eyes sharp—too sharp, too watchful. It was terror that held her still and silent.

Az dragged air into his lungs and pumped his legs faster. Ev's breaths were loud beside him as they sped around the bright stalls and away from the lantern-strung riverside, racing into the dim warren of alleys and backstreets he knew like the back of his hand. The sweet scents shifted to stale rainwater from puddles, cheap home cooking from a nearby open window, and piss—no matter where he went in the market quarter, it stank of river water and piss.

"Left!" Jaromir gasped, his red hair flashing in Az's vision as his friend streaked past him, racing towards an opening in the alleyway on their left.

"But there's nothing there except..." Evrille began growling, and then swallowed, her husky voice uncommonly stark. "Except the Wolven Lord's graveyard."

Zamanya laughed, a rough sound that usually sent a pang of unease through Az's chest. It was no different now. He glanced between his friends, his little family, and his chest tightened. One of these days, only three of them were going to return. Az wished he could turn it off—his desperate need for revenge, the vicious desire to watch the people who'd killed his parents suffer.

"I like where this is going," Zamanya said with a crooked grin, flicking black braids over her shoulder as she peered back at Ev, her dark eyes lingering on Siofra in Azrail's arms for a second before she whipped forward again, her burgundy leathers creaking as she sprinted down the uneven cobbles.

"I don't," Azrail muttered breathlessly, but he followed her and Jaromir in a mad run into the alley. The hum of Vassalaer fell silent: voices from one of the cafe barges on the nearby river hushed, shouts from the markets turned to murmurs, a shrill argument in a house to their right muffled, and even the gulls' calls were quieter, like a blanket had been thrown over his senses.

There was something about this place, about all the saints' temples but especially the one to this forsaken saint, the saint whose name had been intentionally forgotten, whose story had been thoroughly erased … Azrail could almost believe the wrathful saint himself loomed over them, judging their souls like he judged the dead in his chasm.

"They're coming," Siofra breathed suddenly, her voice light and tremulous as she curled her fingers into the fabric of his shirt, peering over his shoulder. She was trembling, her body a block of ice in his arms. Pure white light burst through her clenched fist and Az's chest caved in as he glanced away, his eyes stinging.

Saintslight. It really *was* saintslight. And to be so close to that mythical power … his knees threatened to buckle as he made the tight turn at the end of the small alley, following the red blur of Jaro's hair and the gold streak of Zamanya's magic.

Stomach already in knots, Az glanced back as they rounded the corner, swearing softly at the burnt orange uniforms following them like a wildfire. He locked down his dread so Siofra wouldn't see it, letting her see only strength as he ran faster, pulling up more and more magic from the earth.

They'd have to fight, and it would be an equal match. The Foxes were all fae, and at least one of them was full-blooded. A match for Az and Ev's demi-fae magic and Zamanya's full power. As a beastkind, Jaro didn't possess any magic other than the spark needed to transform into a jaguar, but he knew how to fight. Maybe they'd have the edge. They'd walked away from fights with worse odds.

But power built in coiling ribbons around the Foxes' spears when Azrail threw another rapid, assessing glance, each breath scraping up his throat as he pulled up yet more power, holding it shaking in his arms. He'd have to give Siofra to Evrille or Jaro while he let loose this coiling strike of magic.

No, he hissed at the clever power that once again opened a lazy eye from deep within him. *Not you. Go back to sleep.*

To his relief it did. For now.

"Faster!" Azrail growled at his family, the full weight of his authority behind the word—a voice he preferred not to use. Rare, for a demi-fae to have this dominance, and rarer still for one to possess this much power—enough to rip up a whole square.

He flicked his fingertips, the only movement he could manage with his hands gripping Siofra tight, that precious cargo. Saintslight ... shit. She could commune with the saints. Or at least was brushed by their power, *imbued* with it. She was the only glimpse of that power they'd seen since the last Ghathanian Queen, since that rare light was snuffed out by the current crown family. No way in the dark fucking chasm was Azrail letting these Foxes snuff out this child's light as well.

Not just because she was a kid and didn't deserve the kind of end intended for her but ... pivotal. She was *so* damn pivotal to the things he planned in secret. She could change everything—for him, for his sister, for every persecuted or indentured beastkind in the Vassal Empire.

He tugged on a thread and the dirty bricks in the back street behind them rumbled, hauling themselves out of the ground. Az didn't look, trusting his magic, trusting the living earth in the stones as they slammed up into their enemies' skulls, into their chests, and between their legs. A messy, brute strength blow with little precision, but Az only needed to slow them down.

"Siofra, no," he gasped as the girl lifted her fingertips, ribbons of pure moon-white illumination trickling from her fingers. Power ruptured through the world, as solid as any bomb's explosion.

Azrail was thrown viciously into the side of the undertaker's house—the only person willing to live so close to the Wolven Lord's desecrated temple—as power blasted from Siofra, so strong that his bones shook, his hairs stood on end, and every atom in his body lit up, as if struck by lightning. Not painful, but the awareness of that power, that pure, undiluted magic ... his senses sharpened.

Everything in him sharpened, honed. His earth magic dismantled whatever was left of the cobblestones, creating an abyss in the middle of the alley that even the rats avoided. He was almost relieved when his heightened magic dropped, returning to his normal level.

"Gone," Siofra murmured shakily, clutching tight to his jacket. And they were. The Foxes were little more than blackened scorch marks on the walls, on whatever remained of the ground. Incinerated from existence. Smited.

"Saints," Evrille swore, looking at Az with blind terror and awe on her tanned face.

He knew what she was thinking: that this rescue was deadly, even for a group of rebels who'd dedicated themselves to saving people destined for the chopping block. Everyone else they saved, the Foxes would hunt for weeks and then forget. But a girl with saintslight ... even the council—fuck, even the *queen*—would hunt her down.

And if they found her, they'd find him and Evrille.

But what could they do? Abandon Siofra now? Azrail didn't have that kind of cruel ruthlessness in his soul. For his enemies, certainly, and for those who'd orchestrated his parents' deaths, but for this scared, innocent girl ... no. There was no abandoning her now. He tightened his grip on her, watching the light fade from her clenched fingers as they all stood there, staring, shaken.

"Come on," Jaromir urged with a gesture of his pale, elegant hand, three steps closer to the graveyard at the far end of the alley. His eyes were bright at the sight of saintslight, but not daunted. "Faster, Az, Evrille!"

Azrail glanced at the scorch marks one last time and hurried to catch up to his friend, Zamanya lifting her palms and sending a streak of golden magic across the alleyway, a barrier that would slow the Foxes. It wouldn't buy them much time, but it would buy them some, and he was grateful for it.

"Everyone alright?" he asked as he ran, his chest tight and strained, aching for breath that wouldn't come until they were safely home.

"Fine," Zamanya bit out, her chocolate eyes churning as she scanned the silent, hallowed place they emerged into at the end of the alley.

"I'm okay," Jaro said, watching Az carefully with jade green eyes that missed nothing. Being observant was a prerequisite of his job—as both a courtesan at the pillow rooms and Azrail's most trusted spy. "Are *you?*"

Az pressed his mouth into a thin line, but he wouldn't give them an honest answer to this, not even to Jaro who knew about the breathlessness and dizziness that struck when he was anxious like this. "Let's just get home. Ev?"

Evrille stalked closer, trampling weeds with her heavy boots as she surveyed the space around them with distrust. The Wolven Lord's temple had once been the biggest in the city, in the entire Vassal Empire according to the few stories and whispers that remained, but now it was little more than a ruin. An overgrown garden flecked with chunks of stone and shards of mirrored copper from its shattered dome was all that survived, marble columns collapsed in the long grass and every stained-glass window blown out. Intentionally, Az assumed, and wondered what the hell this saint had done to become so hated, so feared.

There was no longer any need for a temple to the saint who ruled over the souls of the chasm; not a single person worshipped him. No one remembered his name, not the way they knew Manus, Sephanae, and Enryr, the saints of the ocean, the living, and knowledge respectively. If the Wolven Lord had once had a name, it had been scratched out of every history book, from every scroll of lore and tome of myths. It had even been gouged from the stone carvings on the arched doorway of his own temple, the only part of the original building left standing.

This was a bleak place, hushed and frozen in a way that most of busy Vassalaer wasn't, and that clever, sleeping magic in Azrail widened its eye to cast a look around, responding to the dark power that bled from the earth here.

"Would you check Siofra for injuries?" he asked his sister,

finally dragging his gaze from the ruins and weathered gravestones that thrust up from the long grass like jagged teeth.

Evrille nodded her dark head, still wary as she drew close. "I'm Evrille," she told the girl, her expression neutral and kind—her healer face. While Ev had never received official training—the risk that whoever processed her application would discover her true name was too high a risk—she'd stubbornly helped out at the nearest Hall of Indira every weekend until she was eighteen, when she was invited to apprentice for one of the healers there. Her bedside manner usually left a lot to be desired, but she was one hell of a healer, and Az was fiercely proud of her, especially as she softened her rough edges and smiled at Siofra.

"I'm Siofra," the fair-haired girl replied, her purple eyes watchful.

Ev lifted a hand, green ribbons of power twining around her fingers, and Siofra recoiled, gripping Azrail's neck tighter. His heart twisted into a knot of rage and sympathy. What the chasm had she suffered, these weeks—or years— she'd been held, awaiting execution?

"It's alright," Azrail promised, catching Siofra's eyes and holding the girl's gaze, steady and calm, hiding his own anxiety far below where she couldn't glimpse it. "You can trust my sister. I promise."

He'd made many promises in his life; to his sister, to his dead parents, to the rebels and beastkind looking to him for direction, to the bastards who'd killed his parents by falsely naming them traitors. He'd yet to break a single one.

Zamanya whistled, giving the girl a toothy grin as she inspected a rotted gravestone. "Now you're really part of the gang, if Azrail's giving you promises. He keeps them all, you know? And never promises *anything* unless he means it."

Az was grateful for Zamanya's grin and swagger, for her

sun-bright attitude, because Siofra relaxed and gave Evrille a nod of consent, loosening her grip around Az's throat, just slightly.

Evrille inhaled sharply as her streaks of green power wrapped around Siofra's emaciated body, a storm churning behind his sister's blue eyes as her fingers moved, guiding the magic. It was bad, then, the state of Siofra's health. They'd take care of her, he swore. She'd never know starvation, cold, or suffering again. Never see steel bars all around her again. He swore it to himself and to the saints.

"There," Evrille said, her voice gentle in a way he rarely heard. Surly, often, and annoyed, most of the time, but gentle and soft in this way ... rarely. Pride burst through Azrail's chest at the way she handled Siofra, at the caring smile she bestowed on the girl as she drew her emerald magic back, at that healing magic *at all*—it had been a surprise when she'd first shown a healing talent, especially after the shadow of their parents' deaths had cloaked them all her life.

But he'd tried so fucking hard to shield Evrille from the grief, the suffering, the ... lack. He'd tried to be a good brother, to give her everything she could ever need. He'd failed at times, and he'd been a bastard far too many times when the pressure of being a parent got to him, but ... it was moments like these when he got the sense that he'd done things right, raised her the right way.

Ev caught the look on his face, and rolled her eyes, back to her usual coarse self as she stalked away, her heavy black boots trampling grass and shattered glass alike.

The stones back in the alley sent flickers of awareness down Az's threads of magic, and he stiffened. "They're catching up. Let's move."

The sleeping power in his gut took one last sweeping look around the shattered temple as they hurried past fallen walls and stone pews—and then it went blessedly still. Azrail exhaled a breath of relief. He didn't know what that dark power was, had thought it to be grief for years until he'd realised otherwise, until he recognised it for what it truly was—magic vast enough to sever his mind, tear his soul, and take over his body. Too much power; the kind that destroyed a person. He'd never acknowledged it since, and didn't let it rise for even a second.

"Let us handle them this time, alright, Siofra?" he asked, panting as they ran from the fallen temple and down a twisting snicket on the other side. Scents of fresh bread and roast pig filled the air a minute before the backstreet fed them out into the market, where shouts of hawkers blended with the screams of gulls. Colour blazed everywhere, from the marquee stalls to the strings of lanterns to the bright paintings on the buildings opposite them. "If the Foxes find us, let us take care of it. You keep your power inside, where it's safe." When Siofra just stared at him, Az urged, "Okay, love?"

She shook her head, her eyes going over his shoulder, watchful, terrified. He knew enough of independence and self-reliance to recognise it in Siofra. How long had she been on her own, hardened to life, desperate to survive? He swallowed, and hated his next words, no matter how vital they were.

"You can't use your power, Siofra. If you use it, the Foxes will find us; they'll see it and know exactly where to find us. Keep it hidden for now, keep it safe. If you use it, we'll all be taken back to that square."

To the executioner's block.

He saw understanding in the paleness of her face, the way her fingers tightened on his jacket. It twisted his gut to see her that scared, full of so much dread, but he didn't have time to coax her into trusting the four of them; he barely had time to scare her into doing what she needed to to survive. And *they* survived too, his little family, all he had left after the crown and council took his parents.

"Foxes patrolling on the right," Zamanya said in a low voice, gold power readying in her hands. "Do we engage or run?"

"Run," Az replied instantly, scanning the rows of stalls and tents in front of them, the three Foxes patrolling down the far end near the soap stalls. "Wait. Stop," he said, hard enough that they all obeyed.

"You're insane," Evrille muttered, even as she huddled in close, her blue eyes sharp with wariness.

"No running," he decreed, his mind working fast. Running would only draw unwanted attention. "We walk through the market like any other person here, looking to buy, browsing at leisure."

"You've completely lost it," Ev went on, her dark braid flapping in the wind off the nearby river, her gaze now hard with judgement, disagreement, and—fear. Fuck, Az *hated* that fear in her eyes, but he'd known all along that he'd have to face it when they made the decision to free the people the queen condemned. To bring her palace crashing down around her, her crown and throne in fucking splinters for what she'd done.

"It's a good idea," Zamanya disagreed with Ev, offering a nod at Azrail and unstrapping the long dagger from her thigh, hiding it inside her thick leather jacket instead. "We'll walk through the market, looking at the stalls we pass, like we're browsing for a specific thing, and then when we're out of the Foxes' sight, we can run."

Az gave his friend a tight smile of gratitude, his magic coiled tight within him, ready to leap to their defence should it need to.

"Maybe we'll even spot a gift for Az's birthday," Jaromir said, pulling his hood tighter around his face and giving Az a mischievous grin. "Stubborn bastard still hasn't told us what to get him."

Azrail appreciated the attempt at levity, even if it didn't breach his urgent intensity. "This way," he said, tightening his arms around Siofra and entering the line of stalls, a father and his daughter out to purchase wares, nothing more or less.

It was shocking, how well it worked, how easily even Zamanya's big, bristling form fit into the shoppers. The Foxes didn't even glance at them, and Az fought the urge to scan the bustling crowd around them every other second, paranoia and a relentless need to protect making his skin itch.

"You're scared, too," Siofra whispered, drawing her face from his shoulder to meet his gaze, so much fear and knowledge in her violet eyes. She'd been through too much for someone so young. *Far* too much.

"We're going to be fine," Az replied, giving her a reassuring smile as they squeezed through a gap between a large woman and a harried baker carrying a tray of loaves to her stall. "We're going to be just fine, love, you'll see."

He kept his magic sinking into the ground beneath his feet, too fast for anyone nearby to see the threads of green power drop into the cobblestones and deep through the earth. He'd walked every street in this city, and especially the poorer streets on the north side, more times than he could count, so it took no power at all to tap into the network of stones, roots, and dirt beneath them, to search for Foxes headed their way.

Seven, at least. Ten, maybe.

"Go!" he urged abruptly as Jaro and Zamanya caught up to them in a back street at the edge of the market, but where the chasm was Ev? "Evrille!" he hissed, scanning the crowd around the market stalls, his heart slamming against his ribs.

The network told him the Foxes were drawing in, that they'd got through the barrier Zamanya had erected and were storming through the Wolven Lord's ruin even now. Soon, he'd be able to see their orange uniforms.

"Zee, take her," Az breathed, passing Siofra to his friend and general. "Go."

"Azrail," she warned, disapproval thick in her voice, in her brown eyes.

Siofra was shaking her head, her gaze wide and alarmed.

But there was no fucking way Azrail was leaving his sister behind. "I'll meet you at the house," he promised, and slipped back into the market crowd.

CHAPTER FOUR

"Seven teacakes and a cranberry loaf!" a woman shouted, so loud and so close by Azrail's ear that he flinched away, bumping into a teenager with the put-upon look of someone sent on an errand. She shot him a filthy look, but Az barely saw it, too busy scanning every slim, leather-clad body, searching every face for golden skin, a mouth tight with annoyance, and sapphire eyes as dark as any night sky.

"Come on, Ev," he muttered under his breath, his panic rising with every second he couldn't find her until he couldn't drag even a scrap of air into his lungs. That dark power slumbering in his core widened its eye, paying attention as Azrail shoved through the crowd, desperately trying to not stand out but painfully aware of the ticking clock.

The orange coats of the Foxes hunting them burst out of the little street where Az and his own family had emerged not long ago, their sharp eyes scanning the market. They swore at the crowd of midday shoppers. At least Az blended in, even with a description of him no doubt passing from Fox to Fox. Had they seen enough of Ev to know her description, too?

Az sent a prayer to the saints as he wove his way through the bustling shoppers, holding back the urge to shove people aside now that the Foxes too scanned the market. Saints, it hurt—this slow progress, the fact that his sister was alone in a square teeming with guards.

If they found her…

The memory flashed behind his eyelids as he blinked, brutally sharp and every bit as clear as it had been that day seventeen years ago. His mother had raged until her very last breath, bucking and struggling against the guard who held her down as the executioner swung his blade. Her face had been twisted in defiance and accusation, even in death. Her dark head had rolled off the platform, and the crowd had gasped in horror and delight. His father … he hadn't fought, had gone to the chasm with grace and dignity. He'd searched the watchers as if he knew he'd find Az there, unable to stay away even though they'd told him to run, to hide, to never come back. Az's father had mouthed a single word. *Yvarash.* More than the stars—part of what they'd always told him, what they'd whispered to the newborn girl in the weeks before they'd been implicated, accused, and sentenced.

I love you more than the stars.

A wicker basket slammed into his gut, clearing the memory of that day, and Az snapped his teeth in the woman's direction, his temper a honed edge and his canines threateningly sharp. He wouldn't hurt a random woman, but *she* didn't know that, and she was clearly one of the humans raised with a healthy dose of fear for the fae because she went pale and backed off instantly.

Az turned away, shaking off the ghosts of his parents, the choking grief that had paralysed him for days and had only broken when Ev needed to be fed or changed or held. He sank his power into the ground with every step, urging tendrils of earth to spread, searching for any hint of embers and boiling water and clear, open skies—how Ev had always felt to him, like warmth and fresh air and freedom.

A throb went through the network of vines and roots, and his heart tripped over itself. Not in the market anymore, thank the saints. He could breathe again—in scraps, but it was air trickling into his lungs, and he seized onto the balance and strength it offered. Evrille was several streets away, and following the river to their home. Safe—or safer than him, at least, and that had always been what had counted.

"There!" a reedy voice shouted, and Az's relief turned to ash. Shit. He spun, searching for the source of that voice, and sent a rush of power into the earth, turning the stones beneath the man's feet into a gaping pit, cutting off his second warning shout. Three Foxes had heard his first cry, though, and now they pinned their gazes on Az, two focused with the seriousness of the hunt, and one wicked with enjoyment.

Az spun away and yanked on the strands of his power, emerald strands tilting the cobbles to tip people out of his path, creating a clear road out of the market and reforming it behind himself, blocking the way for the Foxes. But they had their own power. A rumble of storms cut through the crowd, ozone tingling on the back of his tongue, and a flash of cerise light came from another of them. The third Fox, it seemed, possessed enhanced speed, as Az found out on the edge of the market in front of a stall selling candle wax and scented oils. He crashed into the stall's wooden frame with a bark of pain and surprise, a solid weight slamming hard into his side and knocking him off course.

Az grunted in surprise, and then growled as pain ripped through his side, hitting a rib that had been sore for as long as he could remember. He'd landed on it that day his parents had been executed, when he'd run and run and run, not racing from Foxes but from the sight of his father's stare, from the memory of his mother's head rolling from the platform. He'd fallen, tripped over his own feet, and hauled himself right back up and kept on running. Some days, he thought he was still trying to outrun that day.

A fist slammed into his jaw, and Az tasted blood. The Fox was a thin, rangy bastard with mud-brown hair and a sharp-planed face. The sadist. Of course it fucking was.

Azrail drew his legs into his chest and slammed his feet into the Fox, shoving the man away as he got painfully to his feet, wavering on the cobblestones. The man at the stall behind him made a choked sound and stumbled back, either realising the Sapphire Knight fought a Fox in front of his stall, or just fearing the sheer power thrumming between him and this city guard.

He couldn't hear the man's pleas or promises, couldn't hear the gulls or hawkers haggling anymore; everything had gone still and quiet, his senses now focused entirely on his enemy.

Azrail bared sharp canines and struck the Fox, panting through the pain shattering his ribs as he slammed a fist into the man's stomach. He'd been banking on that blow being enough to slow the Fox down, to put some space between them, but the man's speed took Az off guard, and the bastard took advantage of his aching ribs to slam a deadly fast fist into the weak point.

Azrail's cry ripped through the market street, drawing looks of surprise and then fear. *Fuck*, it hurt. Sparks burst through his vision, and all breath cut out, but Az wrenched hard on his power and ripped a tree from the ground to their right, making promises to put it back safely as he hurled the heavy trunk at the Fox, burying him beneath wood and bark.

Stay until I'm gone, he begged the magic in the tree as he hobbled away. *Stay until I'm gone.*

He made three steps before a strong arm slid across his back, bright power sinking into his bones and healing the rupturing aches until he could walk. He snapped an annoyed glare at his sister as she helped him cross the market. They vanished into a side street, swallowed by the darkness of the tall buildings on either side of the path, the alarmed shouts falling away.

"It works both ways, Az," Ev huffed, giving him a narrowed stare. "We look after *each other*."

Azrail panted, the pain still unbearable, but he forced himself to nod. He didn't have the energy, but he'd made a promise, so he reached back to restore the tree in the market to its original home as Ev helped him limp down the alley. One of his ribs was broken, he knew, too damaged for Evrille to heal on the go. He'd have to bear the pain until they were home, which was fine. He'd borne worse pain.

"What happened?" he demanded, his voice a ragged growl that earned him a sharp glare. "You didn't follow us."

Evrille huffed a hard breath, grinding her teeth. "Some woman shoved past me and knocked me onto my ass near the cloth stall. By the time I got back up, I couldn't find you." Evrille's head turned, midnight blue eyes scanning his face, sweeping down his body, her panic clear. His heart aching and tired, Az held out a hand, offering comfort. Evrille placed her hand in his, and he squeezed twice before letting go, knowing her limits after all these years. "You shouldn't have come back for me, you idiot," she muttered, but she couldn't hide her relief that he had, that she wasn't alone, she hadn't lost him. It was a fear that would always be with her, like it was always with him.

"I'll always come back for you," he told her, ignoring the flat look of exasperation she shot at him.

"Then you'll always be an idiot," she replied, scanning the street ahead as they emerged onto the riverside walk, the path lined with houses to their right, streetlamps and a weathered wall to their left, with all Vassalaer sprawling ahead, messy in its contradictions of shining spires and dirty tower blocks, gleaming museums and dark factories. Home.

A knot eased in his chest. Azrail sent a ripple of power through his network of magic beneath the ground, and his eyes slid shut for a long blink as he felt three lifeforms inside their house, two familiar to him, and one bright, shining star that was clearly Siofra.

"Thank the saints," Ev exhaled, speeding up as their house came into view. Az winced as she pulled on his injury, but he didn't protest the speed as it brought them closer to home.

The squeak of the gate opening was as beautiful as any song, the groan of the door just as divine.

"Where the *chasm* have you been?" Zamanya demanded the second they closed the door behind themselves. Az sank his awareness into the earth around them and built a shield as strong as a curtain wall around the house. No one would come close without him knowing about it.

"We're fine," Ev muttered, shouldering past Zamanya and unsuccessfully trying to evade a hug. She made a sharp sound as Zamanya squeezed her, equal parts inconvenienced and comforted. Az laughed through his nose, and held up his hands as Zamanya turned to him.

"No hugs. I've got a broken rib." His friend's expression darkened with wrath, and he knew she was tempted to march back out to the market and find whoever had hurt him. He managed a smile. "I'll be fine, I just need some tea and rest."

"And my magic," Ev added dryly, flicking her dark braid over her shoulder as she threw her leather jacket over the post at the bottom of the hallway staircase and strode into the kitchen. "I'll make a paste; go sit in the front room before you injure yourself."

Az rolled his eyes, but he obeyed, wondering who exactly was the older sibling here. The jasmine, witch hazel, and orange scent of their home worked wonders on his nerves as he sank into the plush chair in the front room, gritting his teeth against the pain as he stared out the lead-paned window, scanning the tree-lined river path and arching bridge beyond it for Foxes. There were none.

"Guess what the hellion did after you left?" Zamanya said with a grin, dropping onto the sofa at a right angle to his chair, her dark face animated and thin braids falling loose around her shoulders. She'd taken off the biggest plates of leather armour, but kept the gauntlets on her arms, the same dark onyx as her skin.

"Do I want to know?" Azrail groaned. He felt rough, like he'd crawled out of the Wolven Lord's chasm.

"She sent a flare of saintslight at a Fox who followed us," Zamanya said with relish. "Took out a whole swath of the road."

Az massaged the ache between his brows, glancing up with a grim smile as Jaromir leant his hip against the doorframe, scanning Az the way Az checked his friend for injuries.

"She's dangerous," Jaro said softly, so it wouldn't carry to wherever Siofra was—in the kitchen with Ev, maybe. "Is keeping her here with us safe?"

"No," Az replied just as softly. "But I don't trust anyone else with her. Siofra … she's not like the other people we've saved, Jaro." He met Zamanya's eyes, too, including her in his words. His two closest friends, his general and his right hand. "She's powerful. She has saintslight. And you know what Delakore and the council will do if they get their hands on her."

They all knew what had befallen the last Ghathanian Queen—not just so her killer could steal the crown but out of fear of that divine power. If they'd butchered a *queen* and put her head on display to this day in the palace atrium, what would they do to a common girl?

Jaro's expression tightened, his jade eyes shadowed. Three of his clients were crown and council, one of them the Delakore heir himself. He knew *exactly* what they'd do, what manner of men they were. "She stays here with us," he agreed.

"And we'll just have to pray she doesn't lead the Foxes to our door," Zamanya finished.

CHAPTER FIVE

By the time Naemi got to Silvan's Music Hall, Maia had already slung back six drinks, and her head was pleasantly fuzzy. She'd struggle to capture someone with her snaresong now if she tried, and it was a relief to have her magic at arm's length.

She'd loved it once, when she was younger and it was fun to convince the goats in the yard to break loose and run riot through the palace gardens, when the worst thing she used it for was convincing the cook's son that he *hadn't* actually seen Maia cram an entire honey cake into her mouth. That was before her aunt brought in a tutor to hone the power, to turn it from a rush of wind through trees, wild and untrained, to a honed spear of air, carving those same trees into pieces. That was how it felt; like she had trees living in her soul, and every hum and song sliced bark apart, withered her soul to ruins. But that was madness, and she was drunk.

"That took forever," Naemi huffed, sinking onto the bench beside Maia and grabbing the glass of sweet wine that had been waiting for her for an hour. "Sorry, princess." Her golden skin and hair shone like a distant sun under the murky light of Silvan's, but her eyes were dull with irritation.

Maia rolled her eyes, her mood picking up at the sight of her friend. "How many times do I have to tell you to call me Maia? You're my best friend, for saints' sakes."

Naemi laughed under her breath, her amber eyes now alight with mirth. Good. After the long, trying day they'd had, it was good to see her friend smile. That smile made her a thousand times prettier, her cheeks rounded and her golden face glowing; Maia marked several men whose eyes were drawn to Naemi and smiled, knowing she was going to invite at least one of them to have a drink with her friend. Naemi never let her hair down, more bothered that her actions would reflect badly on the queen than even Maia was.

But, here in this music hall—and in the library that was Maia's sanctuary—Maia didn't give a shit what people thought or reported about her. This was *her* time, her tiny sliver of freedom.

Maia took another long drink of the bitter ale she'd taken to drinking lately, bored of wine and cider because she drank it so often, and snapped her head around to give Naemi an excited stare as the rusty old band in the corner struck up a familiar tune.

"No," Naemi was already saying, shaking her head, her eyes crinkled. "No way, princess."

"Maia," she corrected automatically. Seven years of friendship, and Naemi still wouldn't budge on the princess thing. Stubborn to the end. It was one of the reasons they were friends, that stubbornness. Well, that and they both liked a drink, both despised the pretty, simpering people of the court, and both itched at their respective roles. At least, Naemi had itched at it when they'd first met; she seemed to be settling into her role as Ismene's lady in waiting lately, and

Maia was glad. One of them should fit in, at least, and she wanted the best for Naemi. She always had.

Maia drained her glass, licked the foam from her upper lip, and gave her best friend a rakish grin, holding out her hand palm up. "Remember when we were sixteen, and we climbed that apple tree in the palace orchard?"

"And I got stuck," Naemi replied drily. "I remember. I was up there for two hours."

"And who wheedled the stable boy into lending us a ladder for you to get down?" Maia asked sweetly, batting her lashes at her friend.

"You," Naemi grumbled, pushing off the bench. "One dance," she relented, giving Maia a stern look.

"One dance," Maia agreed, and grabbed Naemi's hand, hauling her to the bit of cleared floor where people danced. The song's pace increased, getting faster with every verse, and Maia kicked up her feet to the rhythm, several people around her doing the ridiculous dance, too. This dance was a joke that had begun somewhere in Upper Aether, picked up by a merchant and brought to Sainsa Empire, where a bard had brought it across the sea here. It was the silliest, fastest, most manic dance ever invented, and Maia lost her breath with every kick of her feet and every wave of her arms. The combination of ale in her blood and exertion dulled everything to a pleasant blur.

It wasn't healthy, getting drunk after a bad day to blot out the feeling of controlling Sir Valleir, but it was a few hours reprieve, and Maia took that wherever, whenever, and however she could get it these days. Gone were the days when she could run through orchards and stables—but here, where nobody knew who she was—or cared if they *did* recognise her—she could be free, even if only for a dance or two.

Naemi snorted as Maia tripped over her own feet, stumbling into the wall where a framed coin—the first ever earned by Silvan's music hall—dug into her shoulder. A bruise was surely forming. Maia only grinned, breathless and unleashed. She could have sworn the glade of trees in her soul reached its branches higher, leaves unfurling in bright mossy green along their limbs.

A man impressively twice as drunk as Maia stumbled on one of the musician's chairs and came crashing towards her. She snapped her hands up on reflex, momentarily glad for all the extra training queen Ismene had made her take—self-defense, physical combat, sword fighting, and magical warfare for if she ever happened to develop a way to use her snaresong in a physical form.

"Sorry," the man slurred. "Someone put a fucking chair in the way." He braced himself on Maia's shoulders, swaying on his feet. "You're really pretty."

Maia grinned, flicking long silver hair over her shoulder. "I know. Bar's that way, buddy."

He nodded slowly, the motion seeming to make him even more dizzy, and stumbled off towards the bar. Naemi hurried over, practically sober after one drink, and level-headed as always.

"Are you okay? Did he hurt you?"

Maia snorted. "I'm fine. He's harmless." To *her*, anyway. If he even tried to hurt her, she could have him curled around himself on the floor, clutching his head as agony ripped apart his skull within seconds.

"Do you want to talk about today?" Naemi asked, peering into Maia's face, nothing but solemn understanding in her eyes. She was so put together and … grown up. Her hair was immaculate where Maia's ran wild, her curves generous where Maia's were sleek, her bearing confident and calm while Maia's cockiness was drink-imbued. They'd always been opposites; Maia supposed that was why their friendship worked.

She shook her head—and urgently grabbed the wall as the dingy hall tipped and twisted around her, its dark green walls and bronze lamps blurring into smears. "Whoa, shit."

Naemi laughed softly, grabbing Maia's shoulder to steady her. "I've got you, princess."

"Maia," she corrected, squinting as the lanterns that hung from the ceiling swirled into a tornado of light. "And no, I don't want to talk about it. I want to forget it ever happened." And pretend it would never happen again. Pretend she could say no when Ismene told her to addle the next person's mind. Pretend she had *some* semblance of control over her own life.

"Princess," Naemi sighed, sympathy and disappointment twined in her eyes. But those warm amber eyes blurred in Maia's vision, so she pretended to have never seen the look at all. She was doing it again—pretending, lying to herself.

"I need another drink," she mumbled, and took a step towards the bar when a bell rung. "Leovan's hairy cock," she hissed, her upper lip curled back.

"Last orders!" the barkeep shouted, and the band struck up one final song, a loud, jaunty ballad about a sailor from Crystellion Port and his many adventures on the high seas.

"Let's just go," Naemi said, squeezing Maia's arm and attempting to steer her toward the steps up to street level.

But Maia wasn't ready to be done yet. Wasn't ready to go back to normality. "One last drink," she said, batting her lashes at her best friend, and extremely pleased with herself when Naemi rolled her eyes and laughed indulgently, her round cheeks dimpled in a smile.

"Fine, but get me a pack of salted almonds."

Maia saluted and stumbled past her friend, pretending she didn't see the flash of disapproval and exasperation in

Naemi's eyes when she thought Maia wasn't looking. She knew Naemi would never understand what it was like to cut through someone's mind like a dagger through butter, what it felt like to twist, corrupt, and completely rearrange a person into someone else. But she was grateful to have her here, even if Naemi would never quite know why she drank herself into a stupor so she'd fall straight into a dreamless sleep.

The days when she went to sleep sober ... bad. Unbearable.

So Maia ordered another ale and a box of salted nuts for her best friend, and clung to the promise of oblivion for a little while longer.

※

Maia's loud voice rang off the sky-tall stone buildings of Vassalaer's arts quarter, right by the river that separated northside from southside. Her bawdy song was a masterpiece she'd picked up a few weeks back from a very dignified woman visiting from Saintsgarde, who'd turned out to be just as filthy-minded as Maia. "And fair Vella's shock, at the sight of his—"

"Alright," Naemi cut her off, unable to hold back her laugh even as her golden face went beetroot red at the scandalous song. "That's enough of that."

"That's not even the best bit," Maia replied, relishing the sharp wind off the Luvasa as it combed cold fingers through her hair, chilling her hot face as she and Naemi wound their way past marble gallery buildings, columned museums, grand theatres closed up for the night, and the huge, towering opera house with its malachite spires. This had always been Maia's favourite quarter, so full of art and passion and the hush and call of the river.

"Saints, no," Naemi breathed, shooting her a pleading look.

"He laid Vella bare, surprised at how bushy," Maia sang, grinning and beyond pleased with herself, "what laid between thighs, her honey-sweet—"

"Princess!" Naemi laughed, shoving Maia a step as her ears flushed bright red.

Maia laughed so hard she hiccupped and snorted, tears squeezing out of her closed eyelids at the sight of Naemi's horrified expression. The expression dissolved into red-faced laughter as Naemi leant against the side of a gallery and wheezed with laughter.

"So glad you feel free and safe enough to laugh, your highness," a hard female voice snapped, and Maia spun to face the speaker, the world blurring into streaks of light and shadow as alcohol raged through her. It suddenly seemed like a stupid idea to have gotten herself into this state. "It's good to know you're still able to laugh, unburdened by all the beastkind your family have slaughtered and enslaved."

"It's not slavery," Naemi replied, haughty and defensive as she stepped in front of Maia.

Maia blinked, urging her vision to focus as she readied a song to addle their attacker's mind. But the woman *wasn't* attacking them; from what Maia could see through the blurs, she just stood there, her arms crossed over her chest, her clothes a mix of bland grey and mud-brown the same colour as her hair. Not a member of court, not a southsider—not someone with money. A woman with every right to be pissed off at a princess.

"Not slavery?" she seethed, her hands curling into fists at her sides. "My sister is fifteen, and in training for the pillow rooms. *Fifteen*. You would force a child to learn the *art of the bedroom*," she sneered the words, "just because she has an animal form? Because you're scared of what she can do as a ram? I'll tell you what she's *not* capable of, your highness: being crushed underneath some old man's sweaty body while he ruts her and steals what she should *never* have to give."

Maia's stomach twisted, a sick slosh of alcohol and bile. "She shouldn't—not at fifteen."

She couldn't see the woman's vicious smile, but she heard it in her voice. "Oh, she won't be forced into a pillow room for another year, but imagine being that age and having a spiteful instructor rip apart your confidence and teach you to be silent and unmoving no matter how much they hurt you—"

"Enough," Maia breathed, her skin tight, itchy all over. "And I *don't* have to imagine, thank you. We princesses get the same training." Only hers had started at thirteen, in preparation for an engagement that had never come, thank the saints. Or rather, thank the assassin who'd killed her intended while the hateful man travelled to the training camps at Thelleus.

The woman laughed, a mirthless sound as sharp and brittle as glass. "It's not the same. You won't be forced to serve for the rest of your life because of something you can't change. Because a group of people you'll never meet have decided your life is worth *less* than everyone else's."

"The council are wise," Naemi said, her voice nothing like it had been just moments ago. Now it was steely and unforgiving. This woman was right though—their treatment of the beastkind was *wrong*. "They know what's best for us, they understand far bigger things than we do."

"Spoken like a true disciple of evil," the woman spat, advancing a step.

"That's close enough," Maia slurred, the back of her tongue tingling as a song rose. "Let us be on our way and we won't report this."

"Report it?" The woman cackled. There was pain in that

laugh. Maia and Naemi were a convenient outlet, but they hadn't caused this woman's suffering. Staying would only make it worse; they needed to leave. "You're nowhere near your palace now, princess." The word was a barb, nothing at all like when Naemi spoke it. "You're close to the northside, and you'll find that some of the north's cruelty creeps over the bridges."

"Enough," Maia snapped, and raised her voice in a sharp, lilting song. She could have killed the woman, could have scrambled her brain inside her skull, but ... no word she said was wrong. And what she'd told them made Maia sick with disgust. It was injustice—and Maia had loathed injustice for as long as she'd been alive.

But she couldn't openly sympathise with a beastkind woman, no matter how wrong what she and her sister endured was. No matter how savage the indentures were that forced even children into the army or menial jobs or the pillow rooms like this woman's sister. Sympathising wasn't a Delakore thing to do, wasn't acceptable. So Maia swallowed the words she wanted to say like a drop of poison that burned on the way down and sang her to sleep, giving Naemi a reassuring smile.

"Come on, let's go."

She caught her friend's hand and squeezed, Naemi's face a mixture of pale fear and outrage. She didn't resist as Maia tugged her into a run.

She tried to put the woman's words out of her mind as they raced down lamplit streets and around dark corners, the river's *shhh* always in the background. Checking that they hadn't been spotted, Maia crept inside the back door of the Library of Vennh, and despite her best efforts the woman's words haunted her like determined ghosts.

CHAPTER SIX

An obnoxious sunbeam forced through Maia's closed eyelids, stabbing into her eyeballs long before she'd even opened her eyes, and she groaned, rolling away from the light—and smacking into something unexpected with an, "Omph."

"Tell me you're a handsome, charming rake I brought home from Silvan's," she groaned, rubbing the crust from her eyes.

A soft snort answered her. "One of four."

Maia cracked an eye open, wincing as the skylight in the vaulted ceiling continued to assault her. "Oh, don't be so hard on yourself, Naemi. You're wonderfully handsome."

A smile curved Naemi's plump face. "Morning, princess."

"Morning, rake."

Naemi barked a laugh. "I assume we're going to have to sneak out of the attic and down through the library."

"Yep," Maia agreed, pushing onto her elbows and inhaling a long drag of dust- and book-scented air. It smelled like fun nights and even better days.

Dita Fhane, the head librarian who let Maia borrow this

room in the attic, hadn't *technically* specified that she was only supposed to use it during opening hours, but Maia didn't want to get on the stern woman's bad side. She'd been lucky that Dita had found her, surrounded by a pile of books and archived newspapers, obsessively researching just for something—anything—to blot out the memories of her first snaresong.

She'd been on the verge of a breakdown, and Dita had seen something of herself in Maia's mania, without explanation or expectation, she'd given Maia the highest room—an honour, since the room was closer to the clouds the Eversky, saint of the skies, called home. She'd given Maia this attic to do whatever she wished in—read, research, study, or just sit in solitude, in safety. And to say thanks, Maia worked a few shifts in the book-filled rooms downstairs, organising the stacks. But she loved shelving them so much it was like another gift Dita had given her.

Half of the time, Maia used the attic room to stumble up to as night turned to morning, more alcohol than blood in her system, and the world blurring around her. The rest of the time, it housed her obsession, the one thing she completely and utterly devoted herself to, her single passion —if you didn't count drinking—and the only mystery that had held her focus for three years now: who the chasm was the Sapphire Knight?

"I don't know why you're so obsessed with him," Naemi remarked, her warm amber eyes following Maia's stare to the whitewashed wall she'd covered in sketches, newspaper clippings, book articles, and her own interviews with witnesses. There was a path only she could follow, mapped out from question to answer to yet more questions via lines of chaotic blue cord.

"He's a traitor," Maia replied, narrowing her eyes at the three sketches from first-hand accounts, each one vastly different—one was a white man in his forties with chestnut brown hair and wide, pale eyes; one man was in his early thirties with troubled blue eyes, to-die-for cheekbones, and a smirking face that could melt her knickers; and the third man was older, with wavy black hair and a strong nose, his eyes squinting with a dangerous gleam. Maia had her money on the third man. The only common element in the eyewitness accounts was a crescent-shaped scar on his inner wrist. Perhaps the only accurate part of the descriptions those witnesses had given. Maia had searched every pub, every mess hall, every community building, theatre, and dock for men who looked like those drawings. And found nothing. "He's dangerous," she went on, weaving a story even she believed some days. "Who knows what he's going to do next, who he's going to kill next?"

She meant every question, no matter how fascinated she was by him. The Sapphire Knight might have fought against the injustice handed down to the poor, the undesirables, and the minorities, but he was responsible for seventy-two deaths. He was the mastermind behind the explosion of the festival square on Old Year's Night three years ago. The Hunchback Saint's temple of knowledge had exploded, shards of its white dome killing so many on that day, when everyone had gathered to celebrate the new year. Maia's own cousin, Ismene's youngest child, had died that day, and though she'd never been close to the vain girl, she still mourned her. Still raged at the Sapphire Knight for killing her with his reckless justice.

"Come on, then," Naemi sighed, pushing to her feet and stretching her arms over her head, the bright sunbeam making her golden skin glow, like she was a living sun herself. Naemi had always been beautiful, all golden and curvy and full of poise and light. If Naemi was a sun, Maia was the moon, each one every bit as important to the sky. "We'd better sneak out before the library gets too busy."

She was right. Maia hauled herself off the roll of blankets she kept here for such trespassing occasions, and her heart sank at the sight of her beautiful dress now crinkled into a thousand folds of charcoal and orange fabric. Not ruined completely, but definitely battered and mangled. She'd have to bribe Aethan, the head of laundry, to give it special care to restore it to its former glory.

"You know what I fancy?" Maia asked, stretching out her arm to ease some of the soreness in her shoulder. Blanket or no, she'd still slept on the floorboards, and it didn't make for a painless body.

"Every man and woman in Vassalaer?" Naemi replied with a wry smile.

Maia crossed the floor and whacked her friend on the shoulder, her mouth hanging open in outrage. "No, you cheeky bitch. A pork bun."

Naemi moaned in agreement, brushing out the wrinkles in her own dress. It had fared better than the fine fabric of Maia's, and still held some of its original shape in the red cotton. "What time do you think it is? Will there be any left?" The vendor notoriously sold out his entire cart of pork buns by noon on any given day, and by nine on a weekend.

"There better be," Maia grumbled, her stomach gurgling. She stuffed her feet into her shoes, Naemi wrapping her golden hair up in a stately up-do, pinning it with the owl comb she always wore. "Ready, princess?" she asked as Maia grabbed her bag from where she'd left it on the sill of the little window.

"As I'll ever be," Maia agreed. "If anyone asks, we came into the library at opening time to look for a book on the Eversky."

Naemi snorted. "In these dresses? I'm sure they'll believe *that* story."

Maia's lips quirked, but she just aimed for the door, cracked it open, and when she heard nothing, swept her friend out and down the staircase.

They made it all the way to the second floor before they came across anyone, the Library of Vennh quiet this early in the morning. It had to be eight, no later. A good omen for pork buns.

"He's here," Naemi hissed, grabbing Maia's arm as they crossed the walnut floorboards, that divine scent of old books wrapping around them like a hug.

Maia's head shot up, her eyes wide with excitement as she scanned the records room to their right, and then the study rooms to their left. Weaving through the stacks, past the tables and chairs arrayed in the middle of the room, was the most striking, jaw-droppingly beautiful man Maia had ever laid eyes on. And she had laid eyes on him many, many times.

The first time had been an accident—she'd bumped into him while sorting a stack of books for Dita. The second time had been coincidence—he'd asked her where to find the newspaper archives. But the third, fourth, fifth, sixth, and all the other times? Those were purely intentional on Maia's part. She just *happened* to need to place a book on the shelf behind his desk, or by mere *chance* she was restocking the shelves in the room where he perused for a book. It had taken several of those moments for her to learn his name: Azrail.

She glanced into the study room, slowing her rushed walk to a saunter, and let her eyes trail from his chin-length, black hair—sleek and perfect and pulled into a baby ponytail—to shoulders neither broad or slim, but somewhere in between, currently clad in a fine midnight blue coat, and then down his shapely back to a tapered waist and—sadly hidden by the coat—a backside worthy of statues and tapestries. His face, she knew, was beyond devastating, all sculpted angles and severity, his eyes the deepest sapphire blue—but they twinkled and shone brighter when he laughed—and his mouth ... Maia had dreamt of that mouth. She wished he'd come to Silvan's music hall so she could find out what he tasted like.

She could hardly seduce him in a study room, could she? But with the band playing, with alcohol flowing and laughter all around ... there, she could shift closer, could brush her mouth over his—

Naemi elbowed her. Hard. And Maia looked up, her lips curving into a shameless grin as she realised Azrail had turned, and was currently giving her a smug, knowing grin. Maia ducked out of sight, her face on fire and her heart pounding, but giddiness flowed through her blood.

"You were tragically obvious," Naemi said with an amused smile as they hurried down the warm hallway, reaching up to put her earrings back in—simple golden pearls that were timeless and elegant and suited her perfectly. Maia was more drawn to gaudy earrings that resembled miniature chandeliers.

Maia snorted, waving as a librarian caught her eye from the languages room, a class already filling the oak desks judging by the low murmurs of a tutor speaking Aethani. "You can never be too obvious when it comes to men, my dear friend. Subtlety goes right over their heads, the poor things."

She linked her elbow with Naemi's, the boards changing to thick green carpet underfoot, trimmed with golden swirls that Maia had always thought looked like threads of magic. The tight corridors opened into a vast, sunlit atrium beneath the golden dome, bustling activity everywhere as people gathered around the gilded reception desk. Another class from the scholar quarter across the river were signing in, their voices a loud clamour that Dita would soon hush.

Naemi laughed softly, and by unspoken agreement they took the wide carpeted steps at a clip to avoid the plague of students, emerging into the bright, sunlit street just as the galleries and workshops lining the street opened their doors. Maia could already smell the rich, earthy scent of pork buns mingling with the tang of the river, and she savoured the flavour of the arts quarter, her most favourite place.

With a true smile, she guided Naemi down the street in the direction of the library, her stomach rumbling but her mood bright and soaring.

It lasted as long as it took her and Naemi to demolish their breakfast and return leisurely to the palace—where Ismene was waiting with another task for Maia's snaresong.

CHAPTER SEVEN

Nothing. Azrail found absolutely *nothing* of value in the countless books he'd pored over this morning, searching for even the barest hint of a way to keep Siofra's saintslight hidden. Some way to muffle it, to contain it, to stop it bursting out of her whenever she erupted with emotion. It had happened five times during the night, each one a nightmare she wouldn't—or couldn't—talk to him or any of his family about. Not even Zamanya's crooked smile or Jaromir's soft coaxing got it out of her. And any hope they'd had that their neighbours hadn't noticed the white light flashing from their windows was crushed when Evrille ventured out for healing supplies, and their nosiest neighbour casually asked about the light show she'd spotted.

A rare crystal, Ev had told the woman. They'd found it in the attic, and struggled to control the magic within it. Such stones could be harnessed for a thousand different purposes —not least of them healing—so the woman had accepted the story and let Ev be on her way. But Azrail had no doubt the story was spreading, and if the Foxes picked it up, it wouldn't take much for them to put two and two together, and arrive at their door looking for the escaped 'traitor' girl.

"Traitor my ass," Az muttered under his breath, stalking out of the library's grand atrium.

Zamanya was at the cloth market, bartering for thick, impenetrable material to block out the light from their windows. He hoped she had better luck than he'd had with the books. But there was a chance the saintslight would make it through even the heaviest fabric.

Now he was exhausted, and starving, and not even the beautiful woman he'd shared a smile with could buoy his mood. Even if it *did* flatter his ego. He didn't know her name, but he saw her working there some days. One day, he would stay and flirt with her, but whenever he came to the Library of Vennh, it was to find some vital bit of information. Never for leisure.

The world rested on his shoulders, a physical weight Az felt as he flicked up his collar against the mist wreathing the clouds drifting down from the low clouds to veil the pale buildings and churning silver river. Azrail's path curved around the impressive malachite opera house, with its many spires and monoliths—like a towering, green organ that cut the clouds themselves—and through the early morning hubbub towards Sorvauw Bridge. It would be nice, one day, to come to this place because he had a spare day to do whatever he wanted with, to be like the artists sketching the barges chugging up the river, or the tourists staring wide-eyed at the stone archway that predated even Vassalaer, not because death itself was breathing down his neck.

Saints, the idea of spending a whole morning in the library, reading whatever he wanted, with no reason to hurry back to the house … it was a fantasy he wrapped around his mind as he trudged across the bridge. One morning, to read, to *relax*. It sounded like a saintsdamned dream.

And like a dream dissolving when consciousness struck, that idea of a blissful morning scattered as Azrail opened the front door to his home and let himself in. The smell hit him first—jasmine and herbs and home—closely followed by the low growls of Evrille and Siofra in the middle of the argument. Jaro was at work serving a client he hated, and Zamanya was apparently still roaming the fabric market, so it fell to Az to soothe tempers. As usual.

With a sigh, he shut the door behind himself and walked, weary, into the kitchen to diffuse their explosive fight.

CHAPTER EIGHT

Maia's stomach was a knotted mass of serpents as the guard marched her through the pale, vaulted halls of the palace, her nerves writhing and hissing as the guard escorted her through tall, airy hallways. She was marched silently past harried maids and straight-backed staff with equally silent footsteps, the rare bit of sound coming from birds chattering outside the tall, ornate windows and the wayward children who ran laughing through the halls like Maia had done when she was younger. If they noticed their princess being led through the winding golden halls, they averted their eyes so as not to draw the attention of the fearsome weapon at the queen's right hand—or outright stared. Though her aunt did her best to keep any other empire from discovering Maia's gifts—all the better for her to trick them, to addle their minds—she could do nothing against the eyes and whispers of cooks, cleaners, and guards who bustled through the palace mostly unseen.

On a normal day, Maia's thick skin blocked out the stares and gasps, but on a day when she'd been summoned—when she was only ever summoned for *one* reason—the reactions of those people sliced her apart. Her people—they were *her* people. She was their princess, and they feared her. If she hadn't been of noble birth, would they have shunned her like they shunned the beastkind? True, she didn't shift into an animal form, but her power wasn't exactly ... saintly.

Luckily, those thoughts wisped from her mind as the palace guard led her to the private rooms beyond the towering sculpture of the Eversky, the saint's beard as frothy as any cloud, a storm in each of his eyes, and a lightning bolt clutched in his raised hand like a gift—or a threat. Maia wiped any trace of emotion off her face; she was as cold and unmoving as that statue. She was stone and stone did not feel. Even if stone did crack, just slightly, as the gilded door to her aunt's sitting room came into sight. Her *personal* room. She was escalating her attempts to sway the envoys, then.

Maia drew a slow, subtle breath, fixing her eyes on the entwined vultures inlaid in gold on the double doors as the palace guard's gloved hands swept them open.

"Maia Isellien Delakore, Princess of the Vassal Empire, Right Hand of The Queen," he announced to the people already arranged on settees, chairs, and a single, heavily embroidered sofa imported from saints knew where. Each piece of furniture was rendered in deep jewel green tones to echo the colouring of the walls and rugs. An apt colour for her aunt she'd always thought—the colour of envy.

Maia gave each person in the room a bland, pretty smile, marking each one: her cold, beautiful aunt, her snivelling, vicious cousin, slimy Lord Erren, a handful of guards she saw daily—and of the V'haivans only Prince Kheir and Sir Valleir, the merchant Maia had snared yesterday. Both had glimmering wings on display, the merchant's ruby red and the prince's rich copper.

Maia's stomach knotted further, the serpents eating their own tails. This would be an assault, if Ismene had only invited the one emissary they'd already addled and the prince who was obviously Maia's target. She wanted no one here to witness what happened.

It would be bad, Maia realised, her palms pricking with sweat even as she kept her expression pleasant and neutral.

"Apologies for being late," she said, and made no excuses. None would be good enough for her aunt, anyway, so what was the point?

"You haven't missed much," the prince said with a warm smile on his handsome golden face. Yes, this would be bad—to rip into his mind of honour and goodness, and corrupt it to evil so he agreed with her aunt. But what choice did Maia have? She'd disobeyed her aunt once, and had no desire to do it again. The consequences had been brutal, and she'd been a *child*. How much worse would it be now that Maia was grown?

Some might call it cowardice, the force that kept her doing her aunt's bidding rather than speaking her mind, following her aunt's whims instead of her own wishes. Maia called it safety and self-preservation.

"Prince Kheir was just telling us about his plans for a new alliance," Ismene said as she smoothed non-existent creases from her rich orange gown with unnaturally smooth fingers. She *hated* this alliance, whatever it was.

But Prince Kheir didn't seem to notice as he nodded his head, bronze waves of hair swaying, and turned to Maia with a smile that stole her breath. She took a seat beside her aunt, hating that genuine smile on his face, the open hope in his chocolate eyes. She liked him, she realised. Liked his beliefs, liked the way he measured his words before he spoke, and she especially liked the kindness in his smile. She'd never known a prince like him.

"V'haiv would like an alliance between all known empires, a halt to conquering so we can each support each other. There would be benefits, obviously, to trade, and economy. And less resources would be wasted from our armies."

"Speak for yourself," Ismene replied with a wry smile, her blonde head held high on her neck, all grace and superiority. "We waste no resources, as we only win."

Disappointment tightened Kheir's eyes, but he recognised that Ismene wasn't going to budge and just nodded, tucking his pearly copper wings close to his back. "Another time, then."

"Of course," the queen replied. Translation: never.

Her bright blue eyes slid to Maia, and the message was clear: snare him. Maia swallowed the hatred clogging her throat, and gave her aunt a subtle nod, making sure her snare was still deep in Sir Valleir's mind and he wasn't going to give Ismene any trouble.

Maia felt physically sick as she began to hum under her breath, but it was better that she addle the kind, noble prince than suffer the consequences herself. She didn't *know* him after all; she might have put up a fight if Ismene had asked her to snare Naemi, but she wouldn't fight for this stranger. Even if his steady, gentle eyes made her stomach twist as they fixed on Ismene with open curiosity as she said, "Now, I have a matter I wanted to discuss with you away from the lords and other merchants, Prince Kheir."

"I'm all ears," the prince replied with a smile, adjusting the ochre fabric of his knee-length tunic. He was too good for this palace, for the spiders who ruled within it.

"I know you pushed back against the idea of expanding the caravans yesterday," Ismene said, tilting her head and watching him—waiting for submission to slacken his face, Maia realised, and hated herself nearly as much as she hated Ismene. "But I think today, you'll find yourself much more amenable to the idea."

"I doubt I will," Kheir replied, distaste crouching behind his calm and wisdom. "I'm not moved by greed, your majesty, unlike my merchant friends."

"Then by what?" she asked, watching him as if he was amusing—quaint. The tea and cakes they'd been sharing lay forgotten on the low table between them, Ismene focused on her prey.

"By duty, and loyalty," Kheir replied, and Maia bit down on her tongue as she hummed louder, her song twisting and twining, tugging at her heart even as she wrapped the threads of her invisible power around Kheir's mind like a net. A simple ribbon wouldn't work on the prince, she knew. No, he'd require more effort, more magic. "The loyalty I now offer *you* in our truce."

"I have no need of loyalty," Ismene replied as Maia began to hum in earnest, closing her net of power around Prince Kheir's mind and disgusted at herself for every second of it. The one bit of goodness and light to have walked into this blackened palace, and she was tainting it, corrupting him. "Even in my allies. I need only obedience."

Kheir sat back, his handsome face darkening with offense, thick brows slashed low over intense eyes. Maia felt the ripple of that sharp emotion flare through his mind, tugging on the strings of her song's net. She tightened the strands until his mind was entirely hers, until she was able to plant her own suggestions and ideas in his head. But she hesitated. This crossed a line— planting wickedness in his mind of goodness and strength. He was a confusing dichotomy of fragile and strong, unbreakable vows and wistful dreams.

She hadn't come across a mind like this before—one of true kindness and care, and the willingness to do what was right no matter how difficult. Maia was a steaming pile of shit compared to Kheir.

HEIR OF RUIN

"I'm a prince of V'haiv," Kheir said in a low voice. His words—*his*, when Maia should have been controlling him like a puppeteer. "You'll have my loyalty, my friendship even, but *never* my obedience. I owe that only to my parents, to my crown, and to my people."

Ismene laughed softly, and slid a look at Maia.

Maia frantically tightened her net until the strings of power bit into his mind, cut deep, and her tongue vibrated as she hummed more forcefully, adding another layer of silent melody to her complex song. Sweat broke out on her temples as his mind slammed up against her hold, refusing to bend let alone break, and Prince Kheir fixed his eyes on her, sensing, *knowing*.

She wanted to tell him that she was sorry, that she'd *never* have done this unless she had no other option, but she had to look out for herself, and refusing her aunt was the opposite of looking out for herself.

His wings went dull, flat to his back, and Kheir's dark eyes pinched with betrayal as they shifted from her to Ismene to the guards, and finally landed on the merchant from his own council. Maia had Sir Valleir in so tight a grip that he only blinked when Kheir gritted his teeth and asked for help.

"End it," Ismene said, picking up a lightning biscuit and snapping it in half, calmly dunking it into her tea cup.

"What?" Maia breathed, her heart galloping in her chest. *End* it? Ismene had never told her to do that before. End the snare? Or... end *him*?

Ismene met her eyes and held, unyielding. "Kill him. I know your power can do it, Maia. I sense the ability in you, that call to death. Crush his mind. He's our enemy now."

V'haiv would certainly be their enemy if they killed their prince. And that shining goodness, that beacon of hope and strength that called to Maia's darkened soul ... Maia was to snuff that out? End it altogether?

She licked her lip, her mouth suddenly dry, and her heart slammed erratically against her ribs. She was trapped, like the hunchback saint in the stories, stuck between two jagged rocks, with no way out. Maia only hoped she didn't have to heave herself free, tearing limb from torso, like he had.

There were no good choices—either she killed the prince, or she said no.

Instead, she chose a far more dangerous thing. She asked, "Why?"

Ismene's pale eyes narrowed, her smoky brown teaglass rattling hard as she set it on the table before them and turned the full force of her focus to her niece. Maia wanted to shrink into the sofa cushions, but she didn't dare move even that tiny amount. She didn't even breathe. "Because I am your queen," Ismene replied, dangerously soft, "and I told you to."

"You're not," Prince Kheir rasped, his dark eyes flinty as he slammed against Maia's net of snaresong, severing some of the strands of her song. Powerful—he was almost as powerful as Maia. Her head flared, a migraine setting in, and sweat slid down her back, beneath the dress she'd worn two days in a row. She doubted Ismene had even noticed, doubted anything about Maia mattered to her beyond what she could do for the queen. "You're not her queen," Kheir forced out, his teeth gritted as he struggled against her power, gaining an inch of freedom before Maia fuelled more power into her song, her magic pouncing on his mind and wrestling back control. "Ananke Sanvillius is," he spat.

Ismene snarled a wordless sound of rage, and Maia went unnaturally still in the way only the fae could freeze, fear making her a statue at her aunt's dominance.

Gasping down breath when her lungs demanded she take

air, Maia shook, only fear keeping her net around Kheir. She didn't dare speak.

"Ananke Sanvillius," Ismene replied slowly, masking her fury with a dismissive tone, "is my sister. But as long as Maia lives here, in Vassalaer, *I* am her queen."

"Her handler, you mean," Kheir short back, nothing but understanding and rage in his eyes when they drifted to Maia. She stopped breathing, stopped feeling anything except the sensation of his mind shoving up against her net of threads and magic. "She's not your niece, just a tool—a thing you use when it benefits you."

Maia had often thought those exact words, but it burned to hear them said by someone else.

Ismene opened her mouth to shoot him down, but Kheir hurled the next words at her as if they'd been locked up inside him for both these meetings, just waiting to erupt. His eyes were molten chocolate, his power rumbling through Maia's consciousness, through her *soul*, through the whole palace. "I know what you did. I know about the bombs you set on your own people on Old Year's Night three years ago, killing your own daughter, and I know about the traps you laid on Wylnarren, a city of your own sister's empire. The traps that helped their enemies sack the city." Kheir took a rough breath, his beautiful voice like jagged glass, and Maia's grip on his mind slackened in shock.

Lying—he was lying. He had to be. What he suggested…

"The Sapphire Knight destroyed festival square on Old Year's Night," Maia breathed, reeling from his lies.

Kheir was kind—noble. Why would he lie about something like this, a night that had killed over seventy Vassalians? And the defeat of Wylnarren … it was legendary. It had been carnage. But that great city near the Hunchback Hills in their neighbouring empire had fallen because its Lord and Lady had failed, because they acted rashly—not because Ismene had tampered with the traps around the city. "You're wrong." She barely felt her lips as she spoke, a horrible numbness overtaking her.

"*You're* wrong," Prince Kheir disagreed, equal parts steel and softness. He met her gaze and held it, sympathy and condemnation in those warm eyes. Her stomach roiled, bile splashing the back of her throat. "The Sainsan lords circulated false rumours that the queen and her consort—your mother and father—would visit Wylnarren that day. Queen Ismene tried not to topple the lord and lady of Wylnarren, but the *queen and consort*. She wanted your parents dead, Maia. She still does, I'd bet."

"That's ridiculous," Ismene said with a scoff, unruffled by his accusations. Her beautiful, cold face held nothing but patronising disbelief. "Why would I try to kill my own sister, three months after I signed the first peace agreement nonetheless?"

"Because you're crafty, and cunning, and old enough to know how to play these games," Kheir gritted out.

Rage burning a path through her cold at his lies, Maia resumed her song, strengthening her net where he'd unravelled it, gaining a foothold in Kheir's mind. She dove right for a gaping hole where he'd eaten through her power, and realised the trap too late.

Pain cracked like a whip through her mind, bright and merciless, and she cried out, flinching back from the claws that sank into her magic, holding her there.

"I don't want to do this," Kheir said sadly, his gaze moving from Maia to Ismene, hardening as they met the queen. "But unless you release me from this room, I'll crush your niece's mind like she planned to crush mine."

Like *chasm* he would. Nevermind that she could feel his guilt at his actions, vast enough to smother him. Maia wrenched hard, twisting her song into a scream, and her power hit Kheir's magic like a battering ram. The claws ripped free of her mind, leaving gouges in her power, weak spots that pulsed with pain. But she gripped his mind in her net hard enough to weaken him, and got the hell out of there, panting hard when she returned to her own mind, her own body.

"I can't snare him," she choked out, pressing a hand to her head where pain pounded. Warm blood rolled down her lips, dripping from her nose. "He's too powerful."

"Try *again*," Ismene seethed, giving her a sharp look that blurred in Maia's vision.

She panted, blood rolling onto her dress and dizziness swirling the opulent room into a mass of emerald and moss. "I can't."

"You *can*," the queen argued.

But when Maia sent her magic striking into Prince Kheir's mind, she met a shield of barbs and arrows. And gored her magic on their razor edges.

She screamed through clenched teeth, scrambling away from those shards of vicious steel.

"Fine," Ismene huffed. She gave the guards a look as Kheir shoved to his feet, the prince so weak after fighting Maia's power that he wavered. His power might have been strong enough to keep her out, but he was physically shaky, and it was far too easy for slimy old Erren to incapacitate him. Maia winced at how his head lolled, at her own hand in his suffering to come as Ismene said, "Lock him below. Maybe he'll be more amenable to our desires after a few weeks rotting in the dungeons."

Maia watched them drag him out, her heart a tight ball of pain in her chest and her head pounding with a fierce ache. The forest at the bottom of her soul, usually full of light and magic, felt like a withered winter glade, its branches bare and skeletal.

"You've disappointed me, Maia," the queen said. "Go, and consider how to better serve me tomorrow."

Maia didn't need telling twice. She stumbled to her feet, ignoring the way the world spun, and knew that no amount of drinking or dancing would blur the past hour from her mind.

Instead, she went to the healer's hall several floors above, sat on a hard bed long enough to get assessed—injured but already healing thanks to her fae magic—and climbed up to her room to change from her dress to a pair of trousers and a loose top. Without looking back, she fled the palace for her little attic room in the Library of Vennh. At least there, nobody would ask her to kill a prince.

CHAPTER NINE

Maia was still wound up and shaking by the time she reached the arts quarter, so she walked right past the library and headed to the river, needing its sharp wind and clarity. Her body pulsed with pain, especially her head and the place where her magic sat in her core, and dizziness continued to blur through her. But it was starting to fade with every deep breath of bracing air, and if she was lucky, she'd be thinking clearly again by the time she returned to the palace.

She passed the Baton and Paintbrush, loud voices already spilling out of the pub's warped windows despite it only being evening. Someone was singing a raucous song about a man called Willie that would have enticed Maia inside to learn every word any other day. But not tonight. No, she didn't want humour. She wanted … she just wanted.

She wanted the prince's words to stop spinning around her mind, wanted her body to stop aching, wanted to stop dreading the torture awaiting her as punishment for failing Ismene, wanted her magic to be something more than the spooked animal it now was, hiding within her. More than anything, she wanted her actions to be her own, not decided by a queen who only cared about her existence when she could get something from Maia. And deep in the secret parts of her mind that she usually kept hidden even from herself, she wanted to be free.

Some days, especially days like today, she wanted her snaresong to die in her throat. She didn't care that it was an intrinsic part of her; right now she wanted it cut out, like a rotting bit of flesh, so the rest of her might be spared.

She was too caught up in her thoughts, marching mindlessly across Sorvauw Bridge's pale stones, the biting air off the water and the healer's tonic in her system sharpening her mind.

Maia slammed hard into a body of solid strength and muscle, and bounced back, tumbling through the air—but a strong hand caught her shoulder and set her back on her feet before her body could hit the huge blocks of stone that made up the bridge.

"Sorry," Maia exhaled shakily, her body still braced for collision, for pain. She'd learned, many years ago, how to ready herself for a sudden crash of pain, and she fell easily into that instinct now. "I wasn't paying … attention…" she trailed off when she lifted her head and saw who'd righted her, who she'd *run into*.

Azrail. Mr Super Hot and Tempting from the library. The most handsome, beautiful man Maia had ever seen in her twenty-four years of existence. And that was *before* she'd seen him in a sleeveless black shirt, with sweat darkening a strip down the middle and shining on the black tattoos scrolling down his arms. The enticing sheen coated his muscular shoulders like sensual oil, rolling down his forearms, and disappearing beneath the leather bands he had around each wrist.

Her mouth watered. Holy shit.

"It's you," Azrail remarked, a smile splitting his golden face, lighting his blue eyes until they shone like sapphires. Saints, he was handsome. Maia almost sighed, almost wilted against him. "From the library."

"Yes," Maia replied uselessly, still blinking at his saint-worthy body in shock. Azrail released her shoulder and took a step back, giving her a blinding smile as he shoved his hands into the pockets of his loose grey pants. *Don't look at his crotch*, she warned herself. *Don't you even dare.*

"Wait," she blurted, recovering her wits and blinking until her eyes stopped being so glazed with lust, "you noticed me?"

Azrail snorted, leaning back against the pale bridge wall and giving her a wry look. "Did I notice the most beautiful girl in the library? Of course I did."

Maia blinked. Blushed. And then remembered she wasn't a blushing school girl with her first boyfriend. "You charmer," she accused, crossing her arms over her chest and giving him a grin.

"Guilty," he replied, his eyes full of amusement and heat, elbows propped on the wall behind him, all casual grace and sensuality. "I'm Azrail."

"Maia," she replied, and wondered if she should have lied only when the name hovered between them. But there were enough people called Maia in Vassalaer that he didn't mark her for a princess. No, he thought he already knew who she was: a regular citizen who worked at the library, someone like him, a commoner.

"It's a pleasure to meet you, Maia," he said smoothly, and caught her hand, bowing over it like a courtly lord to press a kiss to her knuckles. Saints, her skin tingled wherever his lips brushed, her heart skittering inside her chest. With one touch, he'd reduced her to a blushing virgin.

She gave him a knowing look. He returned it with a shameless grin.

Conversations hummed and silverware tinkled below them as a restaurant barge glided under the bridge. Silence stretched between Maia and Azrail, but not awkwardly, more a pause they used to appreciate one another.

"Do you always run on this bridge at this time of day?" Maia asked, fumbling for something to say. Her mind was a constant refrain of *he's here, he's talking to you, he thinks you're beautiful*. And he didn't know she was a princess, so he stood nothing to gain by flattery. Unlike the lords and nobles who complimented her, Azrail was being genuine.

"Why?" He grinned, his face utterly devastating with that amused light in his eyes, that cocky curve to his mouth. "You planning to come back and ogle me tomorrow?"

Yes. "No," Maia scoffed, fiddling with the ends of her silver hair as the river wind set about matting it into knots. "You think pretty highly of yourself, Azrail…"

"Just Azrail," he replied, with a secretive smile. Fair enough; Maia wasn't about to tell him her own surname, either. "And yes, most nights I cross the bridge on my route." He gave her a look beneath his dark lashes. "I wouldn't be opposed to running into you again tomorrow. Literally, if you must."

Maia rolled her eyes, ignoring the flutter in her belly. "That was an accident."

"I enjoyed it immensely," Azrail replied, sapphire eyes dancing. "Certain parts of you pressed into certain parts of me, and it was not a terrible sensation."

Outrage and anger rushed to her face in the form of a dark blush. "You fucking cad."

"Guilty," he replied, leaning lazily against the bridge and giving her a seductive look. Damn him, it was working.

A sudden impulse struck: to grab his face and kiss him hard, pouring every ounce of herself into it, and Maia shook with the effort it took to fight it.

"You really do have a high opinion of yourself," she breathed, even as her hands twitched, desperate to grab him. Her heart pounded hard, blood rushing in her ears and dulling the cries of the gulls.

"You can't take your eyes off me, and you couldn't when we ran across each other at the library." Azrail's smirk seemed to be a permanent fixture on his handsome face, *oozing* male satisfaction. "But don't worry, Maia, it's very much mutual."

Oh, the sound of her name on his tongue … she was going to swoon. Saints damn it all to the chasm and back, she was going to swoon and there was nothing she could do about it. But she wouldn't let him know that.

"I thought you'd be sweeter," she said with honey-wrapped venom, a shiver moving through her at the flash of challenge that lit his eyes. "A nice, studious man. Even if you *do* flirt with every librarian in sight."

"That's not true," he said with a deep scowl cutting his tanned face, emphasising the angles and arches of his features. "I've never once tried to charm Dita."

Maia snorted. Loudly. But instead of judging the sound, Azrail seemed even more delighted by her, leaning back against the bridge wall and gliding a sultry stare down her body. "I don't think Dita's capable of being charmed," she said, locking her body against a deep shudder.

"She threatened to hang me off the highest spire of the library building for reading out loud once," he said conspiratorially.

"That's nothing," Maia scoffed, crossing her arms over her chest and leaning against the wall beside him, watching a carriage rattle its way down the bridge road. "I once shelved a book about the saints' circles in the philosophy section by mistake. She made me sweep every floor in the library for a week. All twelve floors! All seven days!"

"Ouch," Azrail replied, and even his wince was attractive. And when the wind caught his wavy black hair, brushing it over his forehead ... he was so handsome it could kill her. "You win."

"I usually do," Maia replied smugly.

Again that look of a challenge accepted crossed his face. "I warn you, Maia, I'm accustomed to winning, too." His sapphire eyes were exceptionally dark, his pupils dilated. Maia's chest heaved as she drew a breath, and his eyes darted to it, and then to her lips, his own tongue darting out to wet his bottom lip.

Claim him, consume him, a desperate instinct raged inside her.

"Then we'd better not get into any competitions," she replied, her breath catching at the slow smile he gave her. Oh, he was definitely trying to seduce her. Trying, and succeeding.

As if he battled the same force as Maia, as if an inner voice raged at him to claim her, too, he surged forward suddenly. Maia groaned, a sound she couldn't control, as his hot palm rasped along her cheek and his mouth slammed into hers. It was a desperate clash of lips, a kiss of the starving and desperate, and Maia couldn't catch her breath. She didn't even attempt to stop her palms flattening to his thin, sweat soaked shirt, feeling the heat and beating heart of him. Power rumbled through his veins, making her own spark as she moaned.

Saints—*saints*, she'd never been kissed like this before.

Azrail drew back with a sharp intake of breath, his eyes glazed, dark. "I shouldn't have done that."

"No," Maia agreed—and hauled him back to her mouth, her tongue brushing his and sending lightning sparks through her senses. She was more awake than she'd ever been, her skin tingling, her heart beating frighteningly, exhilaratingly fast in her chest.

She was shivery when she finally staggered back against the stone railing, lifting a finger to her swollen lips. "Are you in the habit of kissing strangers?" she asked in a thick voice, even though she'd kissed her fair share of strangers herself at Silvan's.

Azrail laughed, a low, velvet sound that thrummed with seduction. "I'm not sure I've ever kissed anyone like that before, beautiful."

Maia swallowed, and just stared at him, her chest heaving, her stomach full of butterflies. She wanted, inexplicably, to grin, and couldn't hold it back. Azrail laughed, smiling too.

"I'd better continue with my run," he said after a moment, his voice low and sapphire eyes still hooded, "or I'll be late home. I'll see you again, Maia."

"Do you have a family?" she asked, suddenly not wanting him to leave. He was old enough to have a wife and children at home, but he held up his hand to show her the absence of a ring. She didn't let her grin grow further, even if it *was* a battle—but then her eyes snagged on the place where the leather band had slipped up his sweaty wrist, exposing a slashed curve of a scar.

A crescent moon scar.

Maia narrowed her eyes, her heart hurling itself into her ribs. A coincidence surely. It had to be. There was no way the man she'd been eyeing for over six months at the Library of Vennh was the Sapphire Knight. But the scar was exactly as the accounts said, and his face ... while not an identical match, he bore more than a passing resemblance to the second sketch, the smirking man with troubled blue eyes.

Azrail's stare narrowed back at her, confused, not realising what she'd spotted. "What?"

"Hello, Knight," she purred, victory and adrenaline

crashing in her blood. She'd found him. After all these years searching for him, she'd found him by chance. Had literally run into him.

He scoffed, shoving wind-blown black hair out of his eyes. "I'm flattered, Maia, but—"

"Don't bother lying," she replied, giving him a sweet smile. "Your scar's showing."

He wrenched the leather band back into place, hiding that damning scar. "You don't know what you saw. You're confused."

Maia snorted, leaning cockily against the bridge. A euphoric feeling of victory raced through her as the wind tangled her hair. "And you're delusional, pretty boy."

Even though she knew his identity, even though she was a clear threat to his anonymity, Azrail couldn't seem to resist the cocky smile that leapt to his face. "That's handsome man, to you. I can assure you, I'm no boy. Or do I need to kiss you again to prove it?"

Maia flattened her lips into a line, staring at him, this myth made flesh. Damn, he was a good kisser. She'd kissed the Sapphire fucking Knight. Naemi would never believe it.

"Why do you do it?" she asked, the question she'd been desperate to know for so long. "*Why?*"

Azrail's amused eyes hardened to pure, wrathful blue. "Because no one else will, and someone has to."

Maia scoffed, if only to cover up her indecision. Hand him in, or let him go? If all he'd done was free beastkind forced into indentures ... she might have pretended she hadn't seen the scar. But he'd *killed* people; his hands dripped blood, whether she could see it or not. "The Old Year's Night bombing. *Why?*" She snarled these words, Prince Kheir's accusation swirling around her head, as sharply barbed as his magic had been when those cunning claws held her captive.

Azrail's eyes filled with as much rage as hers. More. He

took a step towards her, and another, and Maia backed up, her heart slamming against her ribs even as she recalled everything she could do to take him down so she might run. But her back hit the columned statue of the Iron Dove—the saint of all living things—and Maia was foolishly trapped between the column and Azrail's unforgiving body.

"That had *nothing* to do with me. Nothing! The council and crown spread that horseshit to discredit me. To turn Vassalaer against me." He smiled, all bitterness and hate, and Maia stared, wondering what had happened to him during his life, for his charm and smirks to hide such a seething core. Wondered if she might look like that too, if she ever stripped away the years of pretense. "People supported me back then, agreed with my cause and my actions, and that was a very dangerous thing for both council and crown."

Maia's stomach twisted, again a nest of vipers. She knew her aunt wasn't above lying, or manipulating. It was ... possible. Possible that she'd blame the destruction on the Sapphire Knight to stop a rebellion rising against the crown. But she couldn't accept that Ismene would *set* those bombs, that she'd hand down those orders, accidentally killing her own daughter in the process. Maia *couldn't* accept that.

"I don't believe you," she replied, her breathing fast, hands shaking even as she lifted them and shoved against his shoulders. Unmoving—a statue himself. Azrail didn't budge an inch, pressing her up against the column holding up the Iron Dove. Would the saint of life and souls take mercy on Maia— was she looking down now and watching this happen? What did the saint think of all the lives this man had taken? Then again, she was mated to the Wolven Lord who ruled the dead, so maybe she didn't care.

"Liar," Azrail replied, his lips quirking up and the hatred in his eyes shifting, now a mix of wrath and heat.

"*You're* the liar," she hissed back at him, shoving against him again.

"Promise to never tell anyone my secret, and I'll let you out," he said, the words deadly serious. A vow—that was what he wanted. Dangerous, binding words for any fae.

She could give it, could swear to be silent. But what if he bombed another city square? What if he hurt more people? She needed to tell her aunt and the palace guard. "No," she replied, her voice unwavering, unlike her conviction.

"No?" he repeated, his mouth pressed into a thin line. "Do you realise how dangerous it is for you to know my secret?"

Maia scoffed. "I don't give a shit how much danger you're in—"

"No," he replied, close enough that his breath fanned over her forehead, his scent of leather and tea leaves curling around her tongue. Any passersby would see a couple embracing, not a hostile negotiation. "It's dangerous for *you* to know my secret. Do you know how many people want to know my name? Hundreds. *Thousands*. The most harmless of those would try to bribe you into handing over my identity, but the worst … I'm sure your imagination can conjure up something suitably bloody and pain-filled."

Cold dripped down Maia's spine. Little did Azrail know, she was very well acquainted with the sort of agony he spoke of. She had become intimate with it in the blackest depths of a dungeon, had looked it in the eye and snarled in its ugly face. And survived. But what would her aunt do if she found out Maia knew who the Sapphire Knight was? She'd been terrified enough of what Ismene would do—if she'd summon *him*—just for failing to snare Kheir. This … worse. So much worse. "All the more reason to tell them," she breathed, shoving against him again, hating the fear that crept in, as cold and numbing as any winter fog.

Azrail sighed, and backed off a step, reading something in

her eyes. He still had her trapped against the column, but now she had a few inches of breathing room. Not that she could get a breath in her lungs now Maia was thinking about *him*, the queen's favourite hunter.

Azrail watched her, dark blue eyes churning in a storm of emotions that proved impossible to read. "Telling people won't make you safe, Maia."

She ground her teeth, wanting to go home and deadbolt her bedroom door. "Just let me go. I won't tell anyone—for now."

"Swear it." He exhaled hard, all the anger leaving his expression and his posture changing, threatening to exhausted. "For my peace of mind, would you swear it? Consider it payment for all those times I've given you eye candy," he added with a crooked grin.

"Ugh," Maia muttered, shoving him another step away. "You're insufferable."

"And you're still beautiful," he replied. "Just beautiful and deadly now. Will you sentence me to death, beautiful Maia?"

She groaned. "Stop it. Bastard." She cursed, her decision already made. She couldn't knowingly kill someone, and that was what reporting him to Ismene or the palace guard would mean: his execution. Because of her. Not a ripple effect she had a minor hand in, or an accident. A choice. She hadn't been able to kill Kheir earlier, and she couldn't kill Azrail now either. "Fine. I won't tell; I vow it. Satisfied?"

"Well, not yet, but if you'd like to come back to my house…" The grin he flashed her this time was heated and full of suggestion.

"Don't make me punch you in the dick," Maia warned him, crossing her arms over her chest again. Heat flashed inappropriately through certain areas, her pussy not caring that he was a vigilante and a murderer.

He seemed to consider it, and then shrugged his bare,

glistening, muscular shoulders. Saints damn it, her eyes were glazing over again. "To get your hands on my cock, I'd allow it."

Maia made a sound in her throat, dragging her eyes away from him, and instead looking over the straight line of the Luvasa, the strings of lights crisscrossing the river streets like a drunk glow worm. "You could be lying about not setting those bombs."

"I could be," he agreed quietly, "but I'm not."

She didn't want to believe him. She selfishly wanted him to be lying, because if *this* was true ... her aunt had tried to assassinate Maia's parents. She might have moved to Vassalaer too young to remember her mother and father beyond a faint memory of leather, silk, and sandalwood perfume, but that didn't change the fact that she was their daughter, and they were her parents.

"We can talk more about it tomorrow, if you come back to this bridge at the same time."

"We'll see," Maia replied, the adrenaline and confrontation wearing off to reveal something brittle underneath.

"Why were you so distracted?" he asked, his sapphire eyes seeing too much. "When you ran into me, you looked a million towns away."

"That's none of your business," Maia replied, equal parts tired and cutting. She turned away, but spun back to face him after one step. "If you harm a single person, Knight, I won't hesitate to sell you out to anyone who comes asking, whether that's a baker, a librarian, or a queen. Vow or no vow, I'll find a way."

Azrail's expression darkened, his tan face pinched with reproach, but he nodded. "I don't hurt anyone if I can help it. Unless they attack me first," he added, "and you can hardly hold an act of self defense against me."

Maia gave him a tight smile, and knew her anger was less

at him than at her own messed up self. Too many lies and truth—her aunt's, Prince Kheir's, and now Azrail's, the Sapphire Knight's. "You'll find that I can, in fact, hold that against you."

"It's not just me you consign to death," Azrail said suddenly, holding her gaze. Unforgiving—dangerous. "You asked if I have a family. I don't have children, but I have people who rely on me, who I care for. If you give anyone my name along with the Sapphire Knight's, you're taking them to the executioner's block, too."

"And what about the victims of your next attack?" Maia asked softly, her words almost carried off on the wind over the Luvasa. "What about them? Shouldn't I consider the lives I could spare by throwing you into Lady Justice's arms?"

Azrail just shook his dark head, either in anger or exasperation. "Believe what you want, Maia, but look into my eyes when I say this, and tell me you still think I'm lying. I have spent years freeing those wrongfully sentenced to death, getting beastkind out of their indentured bonds, and relocating people who'd be put to labour work or sent to the Wolven Lord's black chasm. But I have not, nor will I *ever*, set a bomb in a square full of people, just to prove a point, or out of spite, or whatever other reason people say I did it for."

Maia swallowed. Let her shoulders drop, a sigh leaving her. "Go," she said, waving a tired hand. "Go, Azrail, before I change my mind and shout for guards here and now."

He gave her a long, measuring look, shaking his head in judgement, and took a backwards step. "Is it stubbornness or fear?"

"*Excuse* me?" she snapped.

"That keeps you lying to yourself. I'm curious." He watched her in a way that told her he saw everything. But not *everything*—he didn't know she was a princess, or a tool of the queen, didn't know anything about the things she did, was *made* to do.

"Don't think you know a damn thing about me, *Knight*," she hissed, and turned her back on him. She halted after a few steps, and slid into the shadow of the Salt King's statue, the saint of the sea keeping her hidden as she watched Azrail cross the bridge at a fast, annoyed clip. She leant around the column to see him take the steep steps down to the riverside, and followed him with her eyes to a cobalt blue door five houses down. She only left the shadows when he'd vanished inside.

She had everything she needed to hand him in: his name, his description, and his address.

But did she *want* to hand him in? Or did she want to interrogate him for the answers to every question she'd built up over the years?

She didn't know. Even trudging back across the bridge and through the arts quarter to the library, scaling the floors to her attic room where she stared at that wall of questions and answers … she didn't know what she wanted to do.

CHAPTER TEN

The entire next day was hell. Every voice on the riverside path outside the house made Azrail tense, every rattle of a cart on the bridge at the end of the street was a score of Foxes coming to arrest him, every shout from the barges on the water weren't innocent calls, but a capture in the beginning stages, a net ready to close around him. He should have run, should have put some distance between him and his home so Ev, Siofra, Zamanya, and Jaromir might go uncaptured—but he couldn't leave them. *Wouldn't* leave Evrille when he knew losing him, her last tie to their blood family, was one of her biggest fears. She'd had nightmares about it as a child, losing him like she'd lost their parents when she was too young to remember it. He refused to bring those nightmares back to her.

Plus, he had Maia's vow; there was a chance she wouldn't break it to turn him in. She'd started to doubt the version of truth she'd been told—he'd seen it in her golden eyes, the colour of burnished sunlight. Part of her knew Azrail hadn't set those bombs on Old Year's Night; part of her *believed* him. And he prayed that part of her held her silent as he forced himself through his day, making a huge vat of fragrant vegetable stew just for something—anything—to occupy himself with. Evrille knew something was wrong, and even Siofra was watching him funny, like she could tell he was stressed, but he just assured them both that everything was okay, that as long as Sio didn't use her magic, they were hidden.

He was itchy and jumpy by the time it reached five in the evening, the sun just starting to dip as he changed into his running clothes, making Siofra promise not to get on Ev's nerves too much. She only agreed when he let her run a bath, sinking neck-deep into the steaming water with a grin.

Now, with the wind biting at his arms, Az kept an eye on the bridge as he jogged up and down the tree-lined path beside the Luvasa, the exertion loosening his tense muscles. He dragged lungfuls of sharp, musky air into his lungs as his feet pounded the paving stones, trying to steady his mind, to prepare for the battle of wills that was sure to come when Maia arrived.

But she never did. Azrail watched Sorvauw Bridge for an hour, the air getting colder, the sky darker, but Maia never turned up.

Neither did the Foxes—or worse, the palace guard—so he told himself it was a good thing that she'd stayed away, that it meant her conviction that he was a villain was wearing thin.

But it would have been nice to be able to plead his case to her, to try and set his mind at ease that Foxes weren't *actually* going to turn up in the middle of the night. He was terrified they would haul his family out into the street and hew their heads off there and then, while neighbours twitched their lace curtains to watch.

Azrail's mood only got worse with every dark thought that ran through his head, but he ran until his legs threatened to drop him on his ass. He was forced to lean against the rough stone of the river wall, letting his strength rebuild as he idly watched a library barge sail upriver, it's engine thrumming deeply.

He refused to carry any of this fear and restlessness into the meeting tonight. He owed his people better than that. So he waited for his legs to stop feeling like jelly and ran until he could barely stand, stumbling back to the house and sinking onto their settee with a groan, his mind clear.

The jasmine and sage scent of home was a comfort, as was the velvety texture of the cushions beneath him and the noise of Ev clattering in the kitchen, but his best friend's all-seeing gaze was not.

"What's going on?" Jaromir asked, gracefully sitting in the threadbare armchair, in front of the window Az periodically glanced through, checking the street. The setting sun made Jaro's red-purple hair even deeper, outlining the slim shoulders of his fine black jacket in vivid orange.

Azrail shook his head in reply, resisting the urge to drag his hand down his face. "It's nothing."

The chair creaked as Jaro leant forward, his arms braced on his knees and long hair falling into his porcelain face. "Liar."

Az huffed, wishing Jaro didn't know him so well. He pressed his lips into a thin line, listening to the loud cheers of a pleasure boat sailing by outside, determined not to answer. But the truth had a mind of its own and he blurted, "You've been with me at the library when that woman's there, right? The one with long silver hair and freckles?"

Jaro nodded, thoughts spinning behind his jade eyes as he watched Azrail. "This is about a girl?"

"Woman," Az countered, remembering the feel of her curves aligned perfectly with his body, the need to have her as blinding as the sun. "And no, not the way you think. She knows who I am, Jaro. My bands slipped down, and she saw my scar." He ran a finger over the thick leather, the only thing that hid that damning mark. "I don't know if she's going to tell anyone—she threatened to, but I'm not sure she meant it. I got her to vow to keep it secret, but..."

Jaromir swore softly, his tall body as straight as an arrow in his chair and his face draining of colour. "We need to leave. Now."

"She's had a whole day to report me," Az admitted, bracing for his friend's reaction.

Jaro blinked, and blinked again. His jade green eyes narrowed with almost concealed anger. "All day—you've had *all day* to warn us?"

Az blew out a hard breath, dragging a hand through his thick hair and tugging on the ends. "I know I'm a bastard, you don't have to tell me," he said miserably.

"Why?" Jaro asked, softer now as he read Azrail's expression, his elfin face still tight with worry. Az's fault—that worry was *his* doing. If he hadn't flirted with Maia, they'd be safe. But staying away from her was like fighting the sweep of the tide—impossible. "Why keep this from us, Az? You know Zamanya could come up with an evacuation plan in two seconds flat."

"I know," Az murmured, shoving out of his seat and going to the liquor cabinet in the corner. The rattle of glasses sawed his nerves to ribbons as he poured himself a large drink. "If I knew for sure that Maia was going to turn me in, I wouldn't have hesitated."

"Maia," Jaro repeated, picking at the crimson embroidery on his sleeve. "that's the name of this woman who's got us by the balls?"

Azrail nodded, feeling like utter shit for doing this to his friend, to all of them. He knocked back his drink in three swallows, not fond of the burn but enduring it, deserving *something* for risking his family's freedom at least. "I don't think she'll tell anyone, Jaro."

"It's a damn lot to risk on your intuition." Jaro's pale face was tight with reproach. And fear—that was fear darkening his green eyes. For his own reasons, Jaro *needed* their cause to continue, and he needed this safe haven of a house to escape the little room he had in a too-hot, cramped building full of other courtesans on the southside of Vassalaer. He was one of the highest paid in any pillow room in the empire, but that didn't make him any better treated—it only meant his clients were high powered and came with a title or a rank. The extra money didn't change the fact that Jaro only worked in that sick, sweltering place because of the clamp around his ankle —the indenture.

"I'm sorry," Az said softly, his insides seething with loathing and guilt. He took a tight breath, easing his grip on the glass in case it shattered. "We're *happy* here," he said suddenly, the words forcing their way out like they'd been squatting in the back of his throat, waiting for a moment of weakness. He slammed the glass back on the cabinet. "We're *safe*, or as safe as it gets for two dead fae, a beastkind, an ex-guard warrior, and a girl with saintslight." In a pitiful voice, he admitted, "I didn't want to drag everyone away from this sanctuary."

Jaro shook his red head, his expression softening with forgiving. "First of all, you wouldn't be *dragging* us away. We'd leave, to be on the safe side, and come back if the coast was clear. Secondly, you don't hand down orders, Az, that's not who you are. We talk through every issue, and I doubt this would be any different, so it's a group choice. It's not all on you. Thirdly, don't be so maudlin. We'll face this the way we've faced everything else."

"With reckless abandon?" he asked wryly.

"Together," Jaro said with a gentle smile, nothing but

affection on his face. At times like this Az was sure he didn't deserve a friend like Jaro. He could accept brash, swaggering Zamanya, but the softness and care Jaro offered ... he didn't deserve it on days like these.

Az sighed, checking the glass he'd slammed down hadn't cracked—mercifully it hadn't. "Someone would move in and wreck the place while we were gone, and you know it."

"The bones of the house would be the same," Jaro countered, his eyebrow raising. "Why are you being such a stubborn bastard?"

"Because we need to stay in Vassalaer." They couldn't exactly get revenge on Ismene from another city.

"Alright." Jaro stood, his hair moving like a wine red waterfall as he crossed his arms. A habit that had been trained out of him at the pillow rooms, but Az and Zamanya had corrupted him. "Then we'll find another house in northside."

"Because it's as easy as that," Az muttered. He was being difficult and was fully aware of it.

"It *is* as easy as that for you and Ev, you big grump," Jaro said, crossing the room to grab his shoulders. The touch made Az slump as a bartering ram of relief crumpled his insides. "Now stop being so miserable. I'll tell Ev and Zamanya, and we'll make a plan. *None* of this is your fault."

Az shook his head, but he knew better than to disagree. Jaro gave one last squeeze and left to tell the others. With a deep sigh, Az dropped onto the sofa. His ribs gave a pang of protest, a souvenir from the Fox in the market, but the injury was mostly healed thanks to his sister's healing skill.

He laughed as Siofra plopped down beside him and inched closer, a hefty book in her lap.

"More saints tales?" he asked with a grin, casting off all his anxieties.

"You promised to read the one about the soulmates," she reminded him.

"So I did," he agreed. Azrail balanced Ev's childhood book in his lap and opened to where they'd left off at the only surviving story of the Wolves Lord—his marriage and bargain with the Iron Dove, his mate. Az knew the exact moment Jaro told Ev about Maia because her husky voice exploded with the most vicious string of swear words he'd heard in his life. He wasn't sure whether to commend her creativity or run for the hills.

"You stupid bastard," Ev exploded, storming down the hall and digging her blunt fingernails into the wooden door frame to the front room. As if to hold herself back. Deep blue eyes—his own eyes—glared dangerously at him. "How could you keep this from us?"

"Keep what?" Siofra asked, her violet eyes wide with curiosity but her shoulders beginning to shrink inward at Ev's anger. Az put his arm around the girl and gave her a reassuring smile.

"Nothing you need to worry about, Sio," he promised, and gave his sister a hard look. It was so easy to fall back into it—the mindset of a father with a young child to take care of. He'd given Zamanya similar looks when Ev was young, never wanting his baby sister to worry about anything, even if they *were* low on food, or had zero money, or were struggling to keep the house hot enough to avoid them freezing to death as winter set in.

Ev sighed hard, her gaze flickering. The red-hot rage on her face softened just slightly, her grip easing on the door frame. "It's just my brother being an idiot," she said to Sio, and rolled her eyes, downplaying it. Az's chest hurt as his heart filled with pride. "As usual."

Sio didn't look convinced, but she went back to her book, and Az pushed off the sofa, following Ev into the hall. He was sure to shut the door behind himself so Siofra didn't hear, and faced his sister with his shoulders hunched, his heart steeled for the blow of her rage. He'd failed her; he deserved it.

"I know," he said quietly, fiercely. "Everything you have to say, I already know it, Ev, so save it for after the meeting." He sighed, and added, "I'm sorry."

"This woman's going to turn us all in," Evrille shot back, but more subdued than he'd expected. No fiery temper, just hollow hopelessness on her elegant face, her arms not crossed but hanging hopelessly at her sides. Their mother's face—how no one looked at her and knew exactly who they were was a miracle.

"She isn't," Az swore, grabbing his sister into a hug and holding her tight, determined to get that bleak look out of her eyes. Never—she should *never* look like that. He hated it. Being scared, being full of dread—that was *his* job, *his* role, so he could keep her shielded from it. But ... Jaro was right, they were a democracy in their little circle, and he had to come to terms with the fact that Evrille was a grown woman with thoughts and opinions of her own. And she deserved, as much as he hated it, to know the hard things. "I'll take care of it, I'll make sure she tells no one."

"How?" Ev asked, squeezing him once before pulling away, brushing her dark clothes as if some of Az's love and softness might have clung to the fabric like the spores of a disease.

He snorted—she scowled—and balance was restored.

"I put enough doubt in her mind about the stories she's heard of the Sapphire Knight for her to hesitate. She hasn't told anyone yet. And she gave me her vow that she wouldn't; to break it would be agony, and incur the saints' wrath."

"She could be biding her time," Jaro murmured, jogging

down the stairs with his coat in hand. Shit, they were going to be late. And where the chasm was Zamanya?

"Do you trust my judgement?" Azrail asked, meeting his friend's eyes, and then his sister's. A grave, serious question.

Jaromir nodded sharply, sliding his arms into his coat, even that movement controlled and beautiful—trained. "Always."

"No," Ev huffed. But when Az gave her a wounded look, she forced out, "Fine."

A weight fell off his chest. "I looked into her eyes, and saw her conflict. Maia knows I'm not her enemy, whether she's beastkind or fae or human. No matter what she said, she's not going to condemn me. Us."

Ev shook her dark head, but he knew from the surly look on her face that she was giving in.

"Zamanya will want her name, so she can look into her and see what kind of person she is, what connections she has," Jaro pointed out, leaning against the bottom of the staircase as he buttoned his coat. He looked so *courtly*, standing there in his fine clothes with his red hair long and gleaming, his skin pale and perfect, that Az briefly wished they were home—his true home. He'd grown up among the clouds and stars, in a tower on the southside, surrounded by people he'd thought were his friends, but who'd stabbed his parents in the back and handed them to the executioner.

He shoved the memories away. That life was dead, just like his parents. Like his first identity.

"I only know her first name," Az told them, grabbing his own coat off the hook by the door where he'd slung it, buttoning the navy wool over his soft jogging trousers and cotton shirt. No uniform or finery for this gathering—he respected them too much to try to fool them into thinking him a fine gentleman, a fae lord. "It won't be enough to track her down. But I do know she works in the Library of Vennh."

"That'll be enough for Zamanya," Ev said with a grin, leaning against the wall with her arms crossed over the bodice of her black dress. "That woman can find anyone, anywhere."

"And then gut them from neck to dick with a subtle flick of her wrist," Jaro added with a chuckle. "Or in this case, neck to pussy."

Ev made a sound in her throat, her footsteps heavy as she turned and stomped into the kitchen. "Always so vulgar, Jaro."

Jaromir shrugged, an easy smile on his face. "Comes with the occupation, my dear."

Evrille made a show of banging things about in the kitchen, getting together the supplies she'd been preparing all day for them to hand out to whoever turned up tonight.

"You raised a prude," Jaro said to Az, his eyes crinkling.

"No idea how that happened," Az replied with a soft laugh, propping himself against the wall and feeling a rare moment of peace.

"Oh, here she is," Jaro said, waving a hand at the door just as a shadow darkened the window. Az's heart leapt into his throat, a sudden fear that Foxes had found them closing his airways, but that was Zamanya's outline, her long braids, her curves and muscle, and her fist hammering down the door. As usual, she threw it open before any of them could answer it.

"My tits have frozen," she said by way of greeting, stomping her shoes on the wall beside the door. "It's started to snow, have you seen?"

Az hadn't, but that was hardly surprising. It had been fucking freezing when he'd gone for his run. But frosts meant worse living conditions, especially for people who were already struggling. He sighed, and was glad for the vat of stew he'd made to hand out. "Fucking snow," he growled. "Jaro, help me carry this stew, will you?"

"I assume *I'll* have my hands full of Ev's healing crap," Zamanya said, leaving the door open and letting all the damn heat out. Az shot her a look, and she closed it with her foot with a feline grin.

"I'll remind you that 'healing crap' saved your leg last winter," Ev said testily, indeed storming down the hall to shove boxes and jars into Zamanya's arms while Az and Jaro split the vat of stew into more easily transported pans. It would be cold by the time they reached the Brewery, but it was food.

"I'm still not happy about being on babysitting duty," Evrille muttered, flicking her dark braid over her shoulder as she watched them head for the door. "Just so you know."

Azrail laughed, balancing the heavy pot in his hand. "She's just a girl, Ev; you'll be fine."

Evrille's midnight eyes narrowed, glaring at him all the way to the door, and probably still glaring when he kicked it shut behind himself.

Zamanya was right; it was snowing, and heavily too. He only hoped he could stop people from freezing, from starving—his people, the people still loyal to his parents after all these years.

CHAPTER ELEVEN

The hulking Brewery building was fucking freezing at night, but a few small fires had been lit around the vast, stone space, taking the worst of the chill off the main rooms. Az still fought a shiver as he handed out cracked bowls of cold stew and cups of peppermint tea to the throngs of people in front of him. It was a fortnightly ritual, coming to this place where he could talk openly about who he was, about who his parents had been, with the fifty people who still gave a shit about them, still dared to remember them.

It was also the only place where the few free beastkind could gather safely, without fear of being arrested, thrown in a prison cell, and only let out when they took the cuff and indenture. It was a dangerous life of always looking over their shoulders, wondering if their neighbours could be trusted, if their colleagues noticed the claws they'd accidentally shown one time, or the pupils that changed from ordinary green to eerie gold. Az was fae, not beastkind, but he knew something of living in fear and secrecy. A different sort, but the effects were the same.

"There's not going to be enough," Jaromir whispered, ladling stew into a bowl and handing it to an aging woman with grey hair and a fierce, defiant grin. She had a wealth of inappropriate jokes, that woman. Az loved her.

"Psst," she said, giving Az a toothy grin across the beaten up table. Her grey hair was a cloud on her head, her eyes like wicked quicksilver. Azrail was already smiling. "What does one saggy boob say to the other saggy boob?"

Az's laugh burst out of him, even if the mother he handed a bowl of stew to didn't appreciate the vulgar joke. "I don't know, Francille, what *does* one saggy boob say to another?"

"If we don't get some support soon, people will think we're nuts," she replied, grinning from ear to ear.

It took a moment for him to get it, and then Az was roaring, unable to contain the laughter as tears pricked his eyes. "That," he said, "is your best one yet."

Francille bowed, or at least as far as her stooped spine would allow. Her eyes flashed, shifter gold, and she beamed. "I thought so, too. I heard it at the Cock and Crown."

"Why doesn't that surprise me?" Jaromir drawled, his lips quirked as he leant against the table, a prince among shadows and grime. "That place is total filth."

"Total is the best kind of filth." Francille winked.

Jaro chuckled, unable to keep the amused light out of his jade eyes. "Always a pleasure, Franny."

Francille gave them both a beaming grin, clutching her bowl in knobbled hands. "I'll be back with more next time."

"Oh, I hope so," Az replied, giving her his best smile as he picked up another bowl, one of fifty they kept at the Brewery. Thirteen days out of the fortnight, only these bowls and tables occupied the empty, abandoned building, but on meeting nights, it was full of quiet voices and laughter. He made sure no one heard them, that no one noticed the lights from the fires, both his magic and Zamanya's keeping them hidden.

"It's inappropriate for someone of your standing to laugh at those jokes," an aging man said with reproach, giving Az a heavy look.

"Standing?" he asked, feigning innocence as he ladled soup into the next bowl. "I don't know what you mean, sir, I've no more standing than you." He winked, and even the disapproving man couldn't hide his fondness. These people were another family for Az. They had been since the moment he'd stumbled upon the Brewery one night, and found a group of beastkind without indentures huddled in the corner. Those initial people no longer lived in the city, had left or gone missing, but the Brewery was as much a safe place for beastkind now as it was then.

The gruff man rolled his eyes, but he was charmed, Az could tell.

When he moved on, Azrail winced at the worn tears and holes in his brown coat and looked up to serve the next person. He exhaled in relief as he realised the man was the last one. He'd had to scrape the pan for enough to fill his bowl; there were only dregs left.

"There you go," Jaro said, tipping the pan over the bowl in front of him to get every last drop. "One steaming, err cold, bowl of stew. Take care, my dear."

"Thank you," the young woman breathed, looking at the bowl as if it was a gift from the saints. By the rangy looks of her, it was her only meal today. Maybe even this week. Az hated it—the divide. He always had. Had always despised that the crown and court glutted themselves on food, and even threw away any leftovers, while here in the northside, people thanked the saints for even a drop of sustenance.

His parents had sworn to change that, had promised a better city, a better world. Sometimes Az thought that was why they'd been killed, because they spoke up for people that those in power wished to remain voiceless. Most of the time, he knew better. They'd found *something*—about the crown, about Ismene Delakore. Either her advisers or the queen herself had had his parents framed for treason.

Az busied himself with stacking the remaining bowls. Fourteen—too many, far too fucking many. What had happened to the people who used to come for a meal and a chance to socialise in safety? Where had they gone? But he knew the answer to that. They were missing—so many of them. Not just free beastkind, either, but the indentured, too.

"It's the same in the southside," Jaro said quietly, watching Az stack yet more bowls, his tanned hands shaking with rage. Jaro had always been good at reading the nuances and tells of his moods. "I saw a merchant last night who told me his twin daughters had gone missing. They went out last Sunday for a meat pie from the meat market, and never came back. Not beastkind—fae."

Az clenched his jaw, using a rag to clean up the few careless spills on the table, hating each wasted drop that soaked the rag. "Where do you think they're going?"

"A better question is who's taking them," Jaro replied, his green eyes dark as he stared across the room at the last free beastkind as they ate in quiet companionship.

Az's stomach tightened, the thought of someone taking Jaromir sending so much anger through him that the dark power slumbering in his core opened an eye. It scanned the room, dismissed everyone, and went back to sleep, to Az's trembling relief. No matter how bad things got, he wouldn't waken that dark power, not when every instinct warned him away from it.

"I don't want you going anywhere alone," Az ordered quietly, his heart balled up tight. "Especially at night."

He expected Jaromir to argue, but his friend just tucked a

red strand of hair behind his ear and nodded, clearly shaken by the disappearances. Enough of the missing were beast-kind to make Azrail think whatever was happening was linked to those with animal forms, but the fae twins brought everything into question.

He'd think about it later.

Voices rose across the room, rough with anger, and Az exchanged a glance with Jaro. He'd barely taken three steps across the dusty room before the argument became clear.

"I need it more than you," a man was snapping, his voice brittle. "*You* have a home."

"With no fire to heat it, with no windows," a second man fired back, dark with anger—the deep seated kind that came from constant suffering. "I might as well be on the streets."

"Like me, you mean?" the first man fired back.

They were fighting over a blanket, Az realised, and his stomach crashed to the cracked floor tiles. Az half wished the Brewery was still in operation and not shut down and neglected for years, if only to give these men something to take the edge of their pain for an hour.

"I'm sure we can find another in the back room," Azrail offered, the crowd of worried onlookers parting to let him through. He put a hand on the shoulder of each man, hating that they had to argue at all. Hating this entire miserable empire. But especially the queen who let this happen. The need for revenge burned like acid in his gut. "We're all the same here," he said gently, meeting their angry eyes. "We shouldn't be fighting each other."

"Not when there are bigger threats," a raspy female voice added. A tall, brunette woman stepped out of the gathering of beastkind, wearing a purple shawl and dress that had seen better days. Her face, though, had enough smile lines to tell him she'd lived a long, happy life—at least before her fortune turned bad. Mida, his mother's best friend. "Jaenett never came home from work last night," she said, meeting Az's eyes with an unusual mix of respect and anger. "How many beastkind have gone missing, Azrail? Do you know the number?"

"Not the exact number," he replied quietly, shamefully. A twist of pain went through his heart, and he swore it rippled through his soul. He could make sure the people here had food and a blanket, but what could he do about the people going missing? He didn't have real status, just the kind these people gave him with their respect and loyalty for his parents, their wish for what his mother had promised them: a city where beastkind had a place among society, not indentured, but equal.

He gave the two men who'd been fighting a quelling look and stepped back. Jaro had already gone into the back room and returned with a worn cotton blanket, which he now pressed into the cracked hands of the homeless man, squeezing the man's fingers.

"Zamanya will teach you all how to defend yourselves," Az said on impulse, lifting his voice so it carried around the Brewery. He knew Zamanya would agree with his decision, even if it took valuable time away from her other duties. But chasm, when was the last time she'd had a day off, or some scrap of spare time? He could ask the same of himself, of Jaro, even Ev. Everything they did was for this—this cause. Something more, something *better*. The world his parents had seen and fought for. A world where the queen's head was on a bloody spike for all she'd done.

"I'll teach you whatever I'm able, too," he went on. "There's no way for me to track down who's capturing beastkind—and other species too—but I can do *this*. I can make sure you know how to fight, so you might defend yourselves against an attacker."

Mida held his gaze, unbending, and then nodded. "It's better than nothing." Her mouth curved. "Your mother would have come up with the same idea." She caught his gaze and held it. "She'd have been proud of you, Azrail."

Az just nodded. It was better if he didn't think too long about his parents, that he didn't clearly remember their faces or think of their last words. That way he wouldn't give power to the dark force that lived in his gut, waiting for an explosion of emotion to take over. At least, that was how he imagined it: his control would slip, and the darkness would rise and devour him.

"For now," he said, clearing his throat when his voice came out thick, "it'll be safer for you to go anywhere in pairs, or threes. From what we've heard, all the people who've gone missing were alone." He turned, meeting the eyes of everyone he could see. "If any of you want to stay in the Brewery, to sleep here permanently, you're welcome to do so. And if there's anything you can think of, anything you might have heard or seen, that can prevent more people going missing, or find those who have, please don't wait to tell me."

It was a weight, having all those eyes on him, all that trust and expectation. He'd never planned to be a leader, to have a whole community looking to him for guidance and reassurance, especially when he was fae and they were beastkind. But it was his mother's promises that bound them together, and their mutual view for a better city that kept them returning fortnight after fortnight.

"The next meeting," he said, his eyes returning to the woman in the purple shawl, his mother's greatest friend and adviser, the only one of them who still lived, other than him, "we'll bring weapons so you might be armed. But if you can afford to stay for an hour, I'll walk you through some moves that will help if someone tries to grab you."

The beastkind nodded, a layer of both fear and trust hanging over the chilly room like a second layer of neglect and grime. Wind shoved through cracks in the roof, and Az nearly flinched, but he forced himself to smile grimly, to show only confidence as they watched him.

"Alright," Zamanya yelled from the back room, her coarse voice a welcome sound. The entire building seemed to release a long-held breath. "I've got everything sorted into packs. Everyone line up, and I'll start handing out your medicines."

Az smiled at her gruff tone, at how she could never quite hide her warmth and care. She might have been fae, too, but these beastkind were as much her people as they were Azrail's, as they were Ev's and Jaro's.

"Form an orderly queue, you heathens," Zamanya snapped from beyond the open door to the second room, and Az chuckled.

"Not the first time I've been called that," Francille remarked, sending a laugh through the line of people who knew her reputation well.

Az let out a long breath as he watched them, the last free beastkind in Vassalaer, and wished he knew how to save them before whatever was snatching up people stole the rest of them.

CHAPTER TWELVE

Azrail stayed at the Brewery two hours more, and taught every single person who remained at least three ways to break out of a hold, making sure they'd grasped it fully before he moved onto the next person, and the next. By the end, he and Zamanya had taught the whole room full of beastkind how to defend themselves, from aging crone, to mothers and fathers, to young children.

Now, they staggered, exhausted through the northside's lamplit streets in the direction of the river—of home. Az glanced back to make sure Jaro was still trailing them, his friend's jade eyes fixed on the bright stars whirling through the sky, casting Vassalaer's sky-high buildings in shades of silver and grey. Even at night, there were clouds above the City of Skies, fat and fluffy and blotting out patches of stars above the market quarter, dimming the sickle of the moon. But defiant starlight still merged with the yellow magic of lamp posts as the three of them turned along the Luvasa's windswept path. Az was glad for the chill that sliced through his coat into the cotton shirt he wore beneath, sucking cold air into his lungs to chase off the fear he'd seen in the eyes of the youngest beastkind and the unease it had left him with.

His people—whether they were his species or not, they were his people. However it had happened, he was their leader, the one they trusted to do as his mother had promised and build a better world. He tried to deserve the trust, tried so damn hard even though he had no resources, no power, no connections, and most importantly, no damn money to spare. What they did have came in from Jaro's work, Ev's healing, and whatever he and Zamanya could bring in from the fighting dens. Enough to cover rent, food, logs for the fire, and very occasionally to heat the copper pipes that ran through the floors, warming the whole house. Not enough for anything else. Certainly not to bribe a Fox to confess everything they knew about the disappearances, which was what they really needed.

Az would be going back to the library and its newspaper archives, he suspected, and combing through the articles for any hint or clue. Would he see Maia there? Would she acknowledge him, or ignore his entire existence? He found himself wanting to see her, to tease her again, no matter the threat she posed.

"The Wolven Lord is bright tonight," Jaro murmured, catching up to them and throwing an arm across each of their shoulders. "Look, there you can see his three heads."

Az squinted at the sky, but there were only twinkling lights, no shapes among the dark fabric of the sky. "Yeah," he agreed.

Zamanya snorted, whipping around to give him a bright grin, her dark face silvered by the moon. "That's the least convincing *yeah* I've ever heard, Az. That was pitiful."

Jaro rolled his eyes, tilting his red head back up to the sky. "You just lack vision and imagination. There, see those three stars in an arch, that's the side of his body."

Az stared at the bit of sky where Jaro pointed, but all he saw was a cluster, not a three-headed wolf. "I'll take your word for it," he replied drily. Jaro shot him a scowl, shoving Az's shoulder as he let go. Az shoved him back, sending Jaro clinging to the street lamp they passed, squawking in outrage. Az chuckled, at least until revenge sparked in his friend's eyes.

"Why do you think they erased him?" Zamanya asked, her head tilted back, looking at where Jaro had indicated as they ambled down the tree lined path, leaves rustling overhead. "The Wolven Lord, I mean. We know his title, we know he's the saint of the dead, but we don't know his name or anything about him. We don't even know what he looked like, because every painting, carving, and tapestry has been burned or defaced."

Jaro batted a lock of red hair from his elegant face, regaining his balance, and thankfully looking deterred from vengeance on Azrail. "People are scared of what they don't understand, and there's no way to understand death until you've already left the living."

"Very wise," Az quipped, feeling … playful. Light, despite all that weighed on him. Here, dicking about by the river, he wasn't the Sapphire Knight, wasn't his mother's son. He was just Azrail.

Jaro sketched a courtly bow, the very picture of beauty and grace even as he nearly tripped over his shoes. "I strive for ultimate wisdom."

"And when you miss that, you … what?" Zamanya asked, her curiosity about the dark saint turning to grinning amusement. "Just settle for quoting saintsday cookie wrappers?"

Jaro gasped, putting a hand to his chest as they walked slowly down the path, none of them seeming eager to rush. "I've never been so insulted in my life. I'll have you know those words were *original*, plucked from my own genius mind."

Zamanya cackled, the nighttime quiet echoing and amplifying it. "I was the one who bought you that cookie, dumbass. I know what was on the wrapper." She nudged Az with an elbow. "You want to know what mine said? Inner beauty shines brighter than any outer visage."

Az tried not to laugh, but didn't quite manage it.

Jaro snorted and laughed at the same time. "Ouch. Imagine being slighted by a cookie wrapper."

"I'll slight you in a minute, sunshine," Zamanya threatened, but she couldn't stop the twitch of her mouth, or the laugh on the tip of her tongue.

Jaro rolled his eyes, pushing long hair behind his ears and warily eyeing a hawk sat on the wall watching them pass. Jaro had always been wary of birds, hawks and ravens especially. "Nope, I know you love me. You're all talk and no action."

"Oh, I can show you action if you'd like," Zamanya replied in a horrifyingly sweet voice that made Az monitor them avidly, smirking. After a jumpy, exhausting day like today, he needed some of this bickering nonsense from his two best friends. Well, his two *only* friends.

Jaro's body language changed, going liquid and sinuous. "Zamanya," he gasped, a freckled hand on his heart, "I do believe you're propositioning me." He glided across the cobblestones between them and draped himself over her side, ignoring her scowl. "If you wanted a night of blinding passion, you needed only ask, my dear."

Zamanya forcefully peeled him off her body. "You've got one too many body parts for my liking, buttercup." She cupped his face, giving him a faux-adoring look. "And I'd rather keep my eyesight."

Jaro just grinned, as bright as any star, and knocked his

shoulder into hers. Zamanya gave him a long-suffering sigh before she linked their arms.

"Come on, your lordship," Jaromir said, holding out his other elbow. Az laughed and linked their arms.

"Not so loud, you moron," Zamanya chided, streaks of gold magic shooting down the path—checking no one was nearby.

"There's literally no one else here," Jaro pointed out, sweeping a hand at the empty riverside walk, the barges unlit and quiet on the Luvasa. Ahead, even the lamps on the Sorvauw Bridge seemed dim, respectful of the late hour. But just ahead, in a row of darkness, their house glared with deep yellow light. Wasting resources, as always. He kept reminding Ev to put out candles whenever she left a room, but she never listened. Azrail was forever going around and blowing them out to conserve wax.

Weight started to slide off his shoulders the closer Az got to home, a relief that nothing else could beat, and he could almost smell jasmine and herbs, could almost feel the old cushions of his armchair and the heat from the fireplace.

He let out a deep sigh as he pushed the blue door open and crossed the threshold. His relief lasted as long as it took Evrille to peek her head around the living room door and give him a tight look. Her braid was matted on the end, a sure sign she'd been twisting it in worry.

"What?" he breathed, suddenly sick. He made sure the door was shut behind Jaro and Zamanya, diving deep into his network of magic to check for weak points and breaks. "What is it? Foxes?"

"No," Ev replied, sighing and crossing the hallway with her arms wrapped around her middle, clutching a black shawl over her nightclothes. She read the exhaustion on his face and pulled him into a hug, her scent of herbs and lemon settling in his lungs, calming him. He didn't let go for a long while. "It's Siofra," she murmured. "She got worked up earlier, and lost control. Or did it on purpose, I'm not sure. She's a stubborn little bitch."

"Who does that remind me of?" he mused when she stepped away, clearing her throat and pretending she hadn't held on tight to his shoulders.

Evrille knew full well he was talking about her, but with a neutral expression, she nodded. "Zamanya. I thought the same."

"Hey," the warrior growled, locking the door and pulling on all three chains. One had been installed newly today, courtesy of his paranoia and a blacksmith friend who owed him a favour. "You know, I'm starting to think you like me, Evrille. You tease me an awful lot."

Ev scoffed, heading back into the front room, but Az blinked at the blush on her tan cheeks. "You wish, Caliax."

"Calling me by my surname now," Zamanya stage-whispered to Jaro. "She definitely likes me."

Az chuckled. Those two together … it would be carnage and chaos. Possibly in a good way. He couldn't tell, was too close to both of them to form an objective opinion.

"What did she do?" he asked Ev, following her into the front room and stripping his coat off, throwing it carelessly over the back of his chair. Fuck, the heat felt good, working into all his knotted muscles and massaging the tension out.

Ev huffed, crossing her arms over her chest and throwing her feet up on the sofa even though he'd asked her not to a hundred times. Sometimes, he thought he'd raised a civilised woman. Other times, she was mostly feral. "I needed something to keep her busy with, so I asked her to help me with a pain tonic. She turned my best vat into a charred scorch mark on the counter. Used her saintslight and just … smited it. And burned my hand in the process," she added.

Az's stomach lurched as he took a seat beside her, the sofa

groaning. He reached for Evrille's hand, found only unblemished skin, and reached for the next—and found the same.

"Yeah, that's the other thing. She got really upset to have hurt me; she didn't mean to, she just got frustrated when I wouldn't let her handle the boiling water. Because I didn't want her to burn her damn face off, obviously," she added bitingly. She sighed, rolling her midnight eyes to the saints above. "She was crying, and saying sorry over and over, and she just said, 'I'm going to make it better.' And the next minute, she'd grabbed my hand, and saintslight wrapped around it, and I was healed."

Az blinked, staring at her hands, neither of which were burned—the same strong, calloused hands he was familiar with. "It's not just destructive," he murmured, squeezing her hands and letting go, knowing how little she liked physical contact. The long hug likely already took up most of her quota.

Ev shrugged, the movement so flippant that his heart twisted, knowing she felt anything but. He was glad Jaro and Zamanya seemed to be giving them space. "Chasm knows what she can do with that power." She bit her lip, giving him a guarded look. "I think you were right, you know? To bring her here. With that power ... anyone else would just kill her." Her voice was a whisper near the end. "That kind of magic isn't anything like ours, Az."

"I know," he agreed.

"She's not a bad kid," Ev huffed, looking at the curtain-shrouded window, away from him. "She doesn't deserve to be executed for a power she can't control having. She can stay."

"Oh, she can?" he asked, mouth curving as he leant back into the sofa cushions. "I wasn't aware I needed your permission."

She kicked his calf without even looking. "She's upstairs, and worked up. I couldn't get her to calm down, only to reel her power back in. You're always ... good at that. Calming people, making them feel safe again."

Az didn't give a shit that Evrille was a grown woman and eighteen years old; he leant across the gap between their seats and pressed a kiss to her hair. "It's my job."

She waved him off. "Go mother someone else."

Azrail laughed softly, already heading for the stairs. By the sounds of Zamanya and Jaro snickering in the kitchen, they'd gotten into his bottles of potato vodka. He left them to it, and hoped they didn't drain the entire store as he pushed off his exhaustion and climbed the stairs.

Siofra was on the bed in Jaro's old bedroom, pressed into the corner beneath a shelf covered in assorted clutter, with her knees to her chest and her body jerking with sobs. It was the only sound in the otherwise silent room. The bite of her tears mixed with Jaro's scent of vanilla and licorice as he took a rough breath.

His heart crashed, and memories of Ev crying blended over the vision of Siofra.

"Sio?" he murmured, bed springs creaking as he tentatively sat on the edge of the mattress. He reached for her, but thought better of it, letting his hand fall back to the bed, tracing its rough weave. Like most things in the house it was budget and cheap, their few fineries coming as favours and thank yous.

At his careful voice, Sio lifted her pale head off her crossed arms and sniffled. She was wearing a pair of Ev's old pyjamas, but the sleeves were too short, thin ivory wrists poking free, too knobbly for his liking. They needed to fatten her up, but that wasn't an easy task on a shoestring budget.

Az sighed, meeting her watery gaze. He dropped every

guard and wall, letting her see his honesty, his worry. "I know you don't know me well enough to trust me yet," he said. "But I hate to see you cry, love, so I'm offering a hug. If you want it." He opened his arms—and blinked in surprise as Sio threw herself at him with no hesitation, her small body hitting his hard enough that the air punched out of his stomach, a bruise surely forming. "It's alright," he murmured, closing his arms around her shaking form. "Evrille's fine, she's not even mad. She was actually less grumpy than normal when I spoke to her."

Siofra let out a sniffling laugh, gripping the front of Az's shirt so hard the fabric wrinkled. "I hurt her."

"You didn't mean to," he replied gently. "She knows that. So do you, love. It was an accident; we all have them."

"Even you?" she asked, peering up at him, both canny intelligence and naivety in her violet eyes. She'd been forced to grow up too soon, he knew, but was still too young to be secure in herself, to have any sort of confidence.

"Even me," he promised, and tried to forget every accident he'd ever made. Something about having Siofra with them reminded him of Evrille being young and all the fuck-ups he'd made raising her: food too hot that it burned her, baths too cold that she caught a chill, forgetting to teach her letters until she was six, and a million other things he still blamed himself for. He'd been trying to raise a child and work full time back then, plus keeping his identity hidden and staying off the Foxes radar.

Luckily, everyone believed he'd fled the city after his parents' executions, and after searching for him for a year, they'd given up the hunt for the traitor's son.

Now he was someone else, hiding in plain sight.

"Evrille won't hold it against you, and neither will I." Azrail squeezed Siofra's shoulders and gave her a smile, the cry of the wind the only sound for a moment. "What you did when you healed her was a very kind thing."

"I don't know how I did it," she admitted quietly, intensely. She stared up at him, gauging his reaction. "I just wanted to fix it, and ... the magic did the rest."

"Magic's clever like that," he agreed, about to let go until she clung on tighter. "Is this the first time you've healed someone?"

Sio nodded. "But I ... I can turn people to nothing, and one time I ... I jumped over the river."

Azrail's eyebrows shot up, a bright spark of shock cutting through his bleak mood. "You jumped over the Luvasa?"

"No." She smiled, the tiniest thing, but it was there and full of sass and personality. "The Curve."

"Ah." The smaller, offshoot. Still, it was the distance of two houses back to back. "That's a long way to jump, Sio."

She ducked her head, her smile growing as she finally let go of him, curling up back against the headboard. "I know. They still caught me, though."

Very carefully, measuring each word, Azrail asked, "Before you were caught, where did you live?"

Sio frowned, a deep V between her eyes. "With my mama. But they ... they stopped her."

"Stopped her doing what, love?"

Sio shook her head, pale hair flying around her face. She dropped her hands into her lap, twisting them in her pyjama top. "No, they *stopped* her. She tried to keep them there, in the house, so I could run away. I was supposed to run to the Brewery if they ever found us," she said, sounding the big words carefully. "My mama was beastkind."

Az's stomach shot to his feet, and he reeled. "Are you, too?"

Sio shrugged. "Not yet. I don't have an animal, and I think my dad was fae like you. But mama thought I might get an animal when I got older, and she said if they ever found us, I had to run or they'd lock me up."

Or worse, Az didn't say. The thought of Sio working dawn to dusk as a maid or cleaner, her hands cracked and bleeding, her pale hair dirty with sweat, and her eyes empty and dull … he had to exhale slowly to calm himself. He knew there were beastkind children put to work in this city, but had never seen any with his own eyes. If he knew exactly where to find them, he and his family would have broken them free, but they were kept secret.

The pillow rooms … another story entirely. They'd tried to raid them over and over and over, but the complex magic protecting those hateful buildings repelled them every single time. Even Zamanya's gold power and Az's earth magic hadn't been able to get through. But Sio's saintslight…

No. He shut that thought down, refused to use her that way.

"I'm sorry about your mama," he said softly, tracing another whirl in the bed sheets as his throat tightened. "I lost mine, too, when I was young, too. I know how scary it is to be alone."

Sio looked at him, one of those all-seeing stares that made her seem much older than she was. "You're not alone," she said with a smile. "You have Ev, and Jaro, and Zammya."

His mouth quirked at her pronunciation, but he nodded. "You're right. And now *you* have us, too." He squeezed her shoulder and stood, trying not to think about why Sio was free to sleep here, in Jaro's bed: because his friend never used it during the night, too busy at work.

Even now, Az knew Jaro was getting ready to go to work, his shift starting at two a.m. He honestly didn't know when he slept.

Siofra thought about what he'd said for a second, and

nodded. "Now I have you. And her; she's coming too," she added with something like relief.

Az froze, a step away from the bed, and a pang of alarm and unease went through him, both his earth power and that dark beast in his gut stirring. "Who?" he asked, every worst-case scenario racing through his mind. A Fox? The queen? Someone worse he hadn't yet had the displeasure of meeting?

"Your soulmate," Sio said, as if it should have been obvious. She gave him a funny look. "Didn't you know that?"

Azrail shook his head, dismissive until he remembered she had saintslight—and the power of the saints ran in her veins. "When?"

She shrugged, sitting cross-legged on the old mattress and peering up at him, her moon-white hair pooled around her. "I'm not sure. Soon, I think. She's in danger."

"Sio," he asked, keeping his voice perfectly calm even as he freaked out internally. He didn't believe in soulmates, but if Sio had been given clairvoyance from the saints, and she'd seen someone coming to them... "How do you know these things?"

She gave him another strange look, as if it was perfectly normal to know what was to come. "I just do." Her face slipped, doubt and fear rupturing her calm. "Did I do something wrong again?"

"No," Az said quickly, smiling reassuringly. The mask came easy, even years after Ev had grown and he'd taken it off. Or had he ever? "No, of course not," he assured Siofra. "Just tell me if you know someone's coming, okay?"

"I can do that," she agreed, nodding and so relieved that an arrow lanced into Az's heart.

"There's a place here for you, with us, no matter what," he told her, so glad that he'd decided to bring her here with his family instead of finding somewhere for her to stay with one of the people who visited the Brewery, like he'd done with the other two children he'd saved from the chopping block. The saints clearly had greater plans for him, for Sio, and wanted them together.

He'd think about her soulmate comment later, when he wasn't scared of Foxes showing up at the door to drag him to the noose.

CHAPTER THIRTEEN

Maia was ... tired. So tired that a night of drinking and dancing wouldn't soothe her soul, and her attic room at the Library of Vennh was no longer a comfort or a distracting mystery. She supposed she'd have to find a new curiosity to study, to help her forget what her aunt made her do during the day.

In several sessions over the next day, Ismene had her snare a *lot* of people—four times the usual number. Maia knew it was punishment for failing to kill Prince Kheir, but she could do nothing but hum until her throat was hoarse, twist threads of her power around envoys' minds until her magic was weak and empty, and obey without complaint.

She wanted to sleep for a week. Or a year.

The idea that the rest of her life would be like this, full of addling people's minds, *killing* them with her power unless they fought back ... it was a hideous future. And one she'd been entirely resigned to until her aunt had ordered her to crush Kheir's mind. Something had shifted that day, and Maia didn't know how to shift it back, didn't know if she *wanted* to shift it back.

Her self-preservation instincts, honed by years in the palace, had begun to fray, leaving too many complaints and refusals on the tip of her tongue, threatening to break free at any moment—at every moment. Maia was lucky to have gotten through a whole day without those refusals escaping their cage.

As for Azrail, the Sapphire Knight, she'd resolved not to think about him—so of course every waking moment her mind clamoured with his face, his words, and every bit of information she'd collected about him over her years of obsession. Resolving the two people—hot Azrail from the library, and the dangerous Sapphire Knight who had blood on his hands—into one person gave her a headache.

Or maybe that was just a headache from overexerting her magic. Ismene had given up on convincing Prince Kheir to join her campaign for expanding the trade caravans, but she'd doubled down on the rest of the envoys, overworking Maia to the point of pain.

But when the queen dismissed her, smiling as the fifth emissary caved and nodded, agreeing to donate a couple thousand coins to her cause, Maia didn't go up to her room and collapse on her bed. She wound her way through the quiet stone halls in the central wing of the palace. A hush hung over these rooms, and the engraved marble arches and scrolling pillars were lit a deep pink by the setting sun, giving the palace a dreamy feel. It hid the poison and evil of the queen well; from the outside Maia would never think something so heinous could happen in these beautiful golden halls. It even smelled of sweetness and innocence; honeysuckle and marshmallow. It twisted her stomach.

Maia kept her chin high, her gait unhurried, and prayed she didn't look out of place. She kept her head high, acting like she had permission to access the vault at the very heart of the palace as she walked past the palace guard there and let herself in.

Maia's shoulders drew up by her ears as she waited for rough hands to grab her and drag her out. But the woman didn't bat an eyelid, and Maia closed the door behind herself with a sigh of relief. She let the gentle, calming touch of the room she'd entered ease her nerves, drawing a deep breath of fresh air. It tasted of oaks and moss and rainwater—of life. Maia even swore she tasted sunshine.

This space was both holy and functional, all six floors of balconies above her head ornate and gilded, and the perfectly square room was open to the sky above, so the enormous tree of power in the centre of the room could breathe. Its dark branches reached high above Maia's head, gnarled with age and lined with verdant green leaves and delicate pink flowers, stretching even beyond the tallest palace tower and spearing the clouds like one of the Eversky's bolts.

It was good luck if a petal from one of those flowers fell upon you, and even better luck if you managed to catch it in your hand. Maia held out her palm and prayed to no saint in particular, but no petal fell, and the branches didn't even shudder in the faint wind coming from the square of cloud-filled blue sky above.

She rolled her eyes at herself. Even the saints wouldn't be able to help her with all the problems stacking up. She needed back the ruthless obedience she'd had just last week, needed to follow her aunt's commands no matter what they were or how disgusting she found them. She'd caught Ismene's attention now, instead of flying under the radar, and she didn't like the itchy, frightening feeling of someone so powerful being displeased with her. If she kept her head down now and used her snaresong without question, she knew she'd be fine, and Ismene would probably forget all about the issue with Prince Kheir, and yet ... and yet it had changed something in Maia. And she didn't think she could blindly obey anymore, even to keep herself safe.

She growled, a rush of power tingling up her throat, and threads of magic stretched across the room like inquisitive ribbons with no true purpose. The forest in the center of her soul was still withered and wintry, its branches bare and dry, nothing at all like the tree at the heart of this room.

She'd come to access the vault, but now that she was here, her thoughts racing a mile a minute, Maia trudged across the lapis mosaic floor to the benches arranged below the tree. She sank onto one with a hard sigh, the hard, icy steel digging into her back. Not iron—never iron, in this hallowed space where fae had been coming to speak to the saints for so many ages that Maia had lost count. If it *had* been made of iron, Maia's legs would have burned at the first contact, the red leather of her dress intact but her flesh beneath ... nothing but blood and welts. Like all fae, she was allergic to iron, the metal deadly to her kind.

She'd contemplated finding a shard of iron and using it against her aunt, just after she'd told Ismene *no* for the first and only time. After the queen had Maia punished so badly that she hadn't been able to get out of bed for weeks, her still-growing body broken in so many places that the bones still weren't set right in her left arm.

She'd hunted down an iron poker in a disused room, but the burn when she'd reached for it, even through seven layers of fabric ... it had been enough to dissuade her from the idea. And no matter how angry or scared and rebellious she was feeling, she'd never acted on those thoughts, those meticulous plans she'd spent hours making—her first form of distraction, before she'd become obsessed with the saints and then the Sapphire Knight. Not just because of the burns she'd suffer—which she would gladly endure—but because of the consequences.

Queenkiller—that's what she'd be. Kinslayer.

She knew she wouldn't even try to put herself on the throne after the deed was done, not that anyone would support her claim to it anyway, but ... it left her a life of secrecy and hiding and running. A life full of terror and panic, ceaseless and unending. It was no life, she'd decided, and banished thoughts of murder. But now, after the week Maia had had, those thoughts were creeping back. Not to act on, *never* to act on, but ... to take the edge off her rage, to whet the blade of her need for vengeance.

So Maia sat in that holy space, the branches of the tree bowed around her, and pictured how she'd do it. It would be easy enough; Maia had never shown any signs of being violent despite being trained to wield a sword, staff, and spear, to throw daggers into targets many feet away, to block a punch as well as throw her own. If she moved close to her aunt, no one would ever suspect it was to kill her until it was too late.

She cut off her fantasy before it could go any further than Ismene's shocked face, her understanding of *why* as Maia let all the hatred she'd kept carefully hidden finally bare on her face. She didn't let it play out any further than that initial satisfying blow, didn't want to see the guards rushing for her, throwing her to rot in the dungeons, and then hauling her out to the executioner's block in the Salt King's Square. No, she just kept picturing her aunt's shock and understanding, and told herself she could use her snaresong to turn the guards away, to get free in those initial chaotic minutes.

There was a *chance* it could work. Not that it mattered how possible it was; the fantasy itself was the important thing, and the longer she closed her eyes and pictured her aunt bleeding out of her gaping throat, the calmer she became.

A soft brush on her knuckles had her jolting, her eyes flying open, but it was only a velvety leaf, the purest, darkest green, and resting just on top of it: a tiny, delicate petal in palest pink.

Maia tipped her head back and grinned at the tree, at whatever bloodthirsty saint had agreed that Ismene deserved to die, even if no one would ever be brave enough to kill her.

Air poured through lungs that had been tight a second ago, and a weight dropped off Maia's shoulders as she rested her head against the bark, wondering just what saint had given her luck.

Or maybe she was being a superstitious fool, and the saints weren't here watching this place at all. She hoped it was the Star-Heart, the benevolent queen of saints, who became a force to be reckoned with whenever her loved ones were threatened.

Maia picked up the petal anyway, fingers gentle on its fragile velvet skin, and tucked it into the bodice of her dark red dress, rising from the bench and crossing to the wooden racks on the back wall. It was a strange place to keep the most valuable objects the crown owned, but maybe they thought the saints would keep people from stealing.

"I'm just borrowing," Maia said, sending a glance at the tree over her shoulder just in case any saint thought to strike her down for theft. "I'll bring it back."

She scanned the shelves and racks, stopping at an orange velvet cushion that held a dark dagger with deep brown gemstones set in the hilt—the stones formed at the heart of a fallen star. It had always been a strange piece to find in the City of Skies, where the Eversky was most favoured. It had probably once belonged to Saintsgarde, where they worshipped the Star-Heart, but been stolen for its power: the stones glowed luminously whenever someone spoke the truth, and stayed utterly dead when they spoke lies. It was called the Dagger of Truths for a damn good reason.

Maia held her breath as she closed her fingers around the cold silk-wrapped handle and lifted it off its deep orange cushion, letting out an *oof* of surprise at its heft. But no magic blasted against her, no alarm bells pealed.

"Well, that was easy," she muttered, hiding the dagger in a fold of her skirts and nodding farewell at the tree as she aimed for the door.

With every step, every heartbeat she waited for shields to grab her by the throat, for a vengeful saint to smite her where she stood.

Step. Inhale. Her ears pricked for every sound, her heart jolting at a sudden rush of wind.

Step. Exhale. She readied her magic in defense, the tip of her tongue tingling.

Step. Inhale. She kept a close eye on the tree of power, waiting for its long limbs to snare around her arms and legs as she opened the door.

It wasn't until she was past the guard and several corridors away that she realised she'd made it out free and finally released her breath.

She could use this blade to cut her aunt's throat. It wouldn't be worth the life of terror that came afterward, but *chasm*, it would have felt good.

Instead, Maia kept her senses—or at least *some* of them—and she crossed through the snow-veiled palace gardens, honeysuckle and roses perfuming the air as she drew a steadying breath. The clouds were so close up here on the hill that she could reach out and trail her fingers through their soft substance, her fingers coming away slick.

She rounded a shining corner of the building, the brick lit vibrant pink by the dying light, and she grinned as she spotted a maid who occasionally came to Silvan's with her and Naemi on the path by the eastern wing.

"There's a slice of spicebread with your name on it," Lenka said with a swift grin, her flyaway red hair dragged out of her ponytail by the soft wind.

"Tell me there's custard to go with it," Maia begged, her stomach groaning. She didn't know when she'd last eaten; spicebread and custard sounded fucking divine.

"What do you take me for, woman?"

"I could kiss you," Maia replied, matching Lenka's smile despite what she hid in the skirts of her dress, despite what she was about to do. Afterwards, she'd *definitely* need something sweet to eat.

"Ugh, don't," Lenka laughed, turning and walking backwards, no doubt expected somewhere right this minute. "I remember how you kiss, thank you very much: like a fish."

"Hey! I was rat-arsed," Maia complained loudly. "And I thought you were a debauched young lord from Upper Aether who'd promised me a *very* good time."

Lenka cackled. "How disappointed you were to realise you were slobbering all over *my* face."

Maia rolled her eyes. "Princesses do *not* slobber."

"Like a very enthusiastic dachshund," Lenka disagreed with a witch's laugh.

"Oh, go humiliate someone else," Maia growled good-naturedly, turning back onto the path. "And save me that spicebread."

"Maybe I'll eat it myself," Lenka joked. "I'd hate you to slobber all over that, too."

"That's uncalled for!" Maia shouted.

Lenka just laughed, and vanished around the corner. Maia grinned, rolling her eyes at her friend as she skirted the furthest edge of the palace with the towering maze of gardens to her left. She kept a firm grip on the Dagger of

Truths, making sure it didn't show even a glimmer through her skirt. Not all maids were her friends; some would go running straight to her aunt if they realised she'd borrowed an ancient relic. And especially if they knew *why*.

She hovered on the edge of treason with what she planned to do. But she had to know the truth.

CHAPTER FOURTEEN

Maia heaved open a door in the castle's external wall that few people used, a shudder racing down her spine as the wall of magic passed over her. With a quick glance to make sure she hadn't been seen, she began to descend the dark, enclosed staircase.

The magic was so strong that this place didn't even have a guard stationed outside. But the power only kept out those planning to kill the people down in these dungeons, or to aid them in escaping. Maia planned to do neither, so the shield allowed her all the way down the dark staircase until the air sat cold and heavy in her lungs and not a speck of daylight lit her way.

Holding her sleeve over her nose until she adjusted to the foul smell—unwashed bodies and other, sharper scents she didn't want to think about, Maia squinted into the dying torchlight illuminating the dungeon and dreaded what she'd find. Memories rushed up around her like monsters, but she settled her breathing and shoved them behind an impenetrable wall of thorns. She was here, but *he* wasn't; she was safe.

She hadn't known how many traitors were kept down here in the palace dungeons, but her steps faltered in surprise at the sheer number of faces peering through the bars as she moved down the tight aisle. All these people were traitors? Maia tried to keep a count of every grubby face and every hunched body as she passed them, the inmates eerily silent, just watching. Not a single one begged her to help them, but she could have sworn she saw pleas in their eyes, the only brightness in faces caked in dirt. Hate darkened the eyes of a few who recognised her, but they didn't shout at her, didn't even sneer, as if their lips had been sewn shut.

Maia's steps echoed off the crumbling brick walls like an army of ghosts stalking her, the only sound as she searched their faces for fierce brown eyes, searched their bodies for beautiful bronze wings. The count in her head neared fifty. *Fifty* traitors, in a single city. She frowned, the only explanation that they were part of a rebellion, but Maia hadn't heard of a plot being uncovered. It was as if these people had been quietly arrested, one by one.

She walked faster, her stomach churning with nausea and not just from the smell and the silence.

None of the faces she scanned were emissaries or diplomats, no lords or ladies, no high-profile rulers or advisers or even merchants from other empires—no one who'd actually *benefit* from treason. Were these all common people?

Maia halted by a cell occupied by a familiar face, and exhaled a rough breath of relief. Prince Kheir was recognisable even though his gold skin was coated entirely in grime— as if he'd been shoved face-first into the cell's disgusting floor. Maia paled at the blood streaking his shoulders, his neck, at his bronze hair in disarray and wings tucked as tight as possible to his back, their glimmer all but non-existent. It was a far cry from the elegant, handsome man she'd met in

Ismene's sitting room, but at least he had a bucket to piss in unlike some of those she'd passed.

At least he was *breathing*. But some part of her, lurking deep down, went dangerously still at the damage that had been done to him.

Chocolate eyes narrowed as she stood there staring at Kheir, at his battered, swollen face, at the way he kept to the corner with his knees pressed to his chest. She couldn't feel even a wisp of his vicious power that had sent claws hooking into her song, into her *soul*, What the chasm did that magic barrier at the top of the stairs *do?* Suppress all power? Maia reached for her own magic in a blind, panicked grab, humming a rushed tune, and stifled a sigh of relief as power tripped off her tongue. That enchantment only held the prisoners in check, then. Thank the saints.

"I'm going to ask you some questions," she told Kheir, locking her frantic search for her power behind cool competence and a royal mask. She was Maia Delakore, princess of Vassalaer; she knew how to fake strength and brutality, had been doing it all her life. "And you're going to answer them truthfully."

She took the Dagger of Truths from her skirts and held it tightly at her side, one eye on the prince and the other on the smoky brown stones in the blade's handle. It had warmed under her grip, but Maia could have sworn icy magic pulsed from those gems.

Kheir's eyes widened in recognition, but he remained defiantly silent, sitting in the corner.

"Why did you come here to Vassalaer?" she asked in a voice like iron, the mask of cold superiority making her skin itch.

Kheir's eyes flashed with frustration and true anger as he got slowly to his feet, wings ruffling in a sure sign of irritation. He stood two feet opposite her, only the bars between them, and Maia inhaled sharply at what had been done to him, at the wounds and slices all over his body. She knew those injuries, knew *exactly* how each one felt when carved into skin and muscle, and she tried to harden her heart against sympathy but didn't quite manage it. Tried to cripple the panic that threatened to devour her—he was *here*, he'd done this. She needed to run, to run*run*run. Her hands started to shake but she willed them still.

Kheir's eyes flared with a message she couldn't interpret, but he gestured at his throat and then his mouth with angry flicks of his scraped, bloody fingers.

Maia swore viciously, understanding.

The magic around this place was a powerful silencer, keeping the inmates muzzled. But could it withstand a snaresinger?

"I'm going to compel you to speak," she told him, and ignored the flash of anger darkening his eyes, clenching his square jaw. "If you want your voice back, it's your only option," she told him, burying her sympathy. There was only room here for ruthlessness if she wanted to know the truth. She couldn't even let her guilt show.

Kheir curled his long fingers around the bars, gripping them in fists, and stared at her. Just stared. Maia wasn't sure why that look felt like an accusation, but her stomach turned over.

Sweat pricked her forehead as she started to sing, weaving a complex melody that was both beautiful and eerie. The magic coating this place like a hard barrier pushed against her own power, resisting—refusing. She sang a long, haunting note and her power turned to mist, insubstantial and free. She slipped beneath, around, and through the silencing magic, half surprised it even worked as she sang Prince Kheir's voice back to him.

After a minute, she let her song draw to a silent close,

watching the prince as he clenched his jaw and rubbed his lips with a thumb. He'd been stripped of all his jewellery, she noticed. His fine jacket had been taken, too, leaving him in a tunic and blood-stained trousers. He was still striking even covered in muck and blood, his lip split and brow bleeding, and nothing could dim the hard light in his fierce eyes.

"Who taught you to sing?" he asked finally, his voice rough after being kept brutally silent for the better part of a day.

Maia blinked, her interrogation slipping a rung. She had hazy memories of a mother singing lullabies, but that was so long ago, and they were faint. Sometimes she thought she'd invented them herself, given herself false memories so she had something warm and hopeful to look back on. "I taught myself," she replied in a voice that was pure royal—pure Delakore. She held his gaze and refused to back down, as if his question had been a challenge. "And then I had instructors. Who taught you to trap people inside your mind like you did to me?"

"My mother," he replied, leaning against the bars and forcing her to endure his heavy stare. She had the unsettling sensation that those sharp chocolate eyes could see all the way into her soul. "Why are you here?"

"I have questions," Maia reminded him. Her fingers clenched harder around the Dagger of Truths, it's weight a solid reminder of her purpose—and what she really wanted to do with its sharp edge, whose heart she wanted to bury it in. "Why did you come to—"

"No," he interrupted, slowly shaking his head, the movement sluggish. "Why are you *here*? Why do you have questions at all? I've already been thoroughly interrogated as you can see, and your cousin got nothing from me, nor did any of your aunt's guards. It's useless for you to be here."

The word *useless* struck deep, a word she'd used as a

weapon against herself in the solitude of her own mind. As diplomats and courtiers begged her for mercy, as her snaresong revealed truths that sent people to the chopping block, as she condemned and implicated and destroyed people. She was useless. Useless to stop any of it. And worse: selfish, to choose to protect herself over those who couldn't protect *themselves*.

Maia gripped the dagger in a fist and raised it between them, her breath coming harder. "Why did you come to Vassalaer?"

"You *know* why," Kheir snapped, losing patience or interest or both. "I thought the queen might join a new alliance." He laughed, a coiling, bitter thing. "I was mistaken." He caught her gaze, and stared deep. Missing nothing. Seeing everything. Maia could have sworn she *felt* his disgust and fear, that the tiniest bit of sympathy and admiration swirled through it like ink through water. The prison was getting to her, fucking with her. "You must be very good at what you do," he went on. "There isn't a single rumour of Queen Ismene twisting the minds of her enemies. Not even whispers. Your work is so thorough, I assume, that even when people return to their homelands, they don't even realise what you've done."

He wasn't wrong. She shut it out. It wasn't relevant.

"Did you come here to turn Vassalaer against our queen?" she went on, reciting the questions she'd memorised. She needed to know why—*why* he'd say things like he had, why he'd lie about something so important. Kheir didn't seem like the kind of person to lie just for kicks or to cause chaos, so ... why?

Kheir gave her a pitying look that made Maia's hackles rise. "No. I came for the treaty."

Truth, all truth: the stones glowing faintly in the sword

confirmed what Maia already sensed. There was no malice in his grimy face, no duplicity in his striking eyes.

"Why would you lie like that?" she breathed, and lost her grip on the Delakore mask, the frantic, terrified truth of herself slipping free. "What do you have to gain from spreading lies? Why would you *say* that shit?"

She'd thought she understood him, knew what sort of person Kheir was, and the lies both damaged her ego to be wrong but ... hurt for a reason she couldn't place.

"I have nothing to gain," he replied, still giving her that look, like he was weighing her soul. The stones glowed true, and Maia's stomach plummeted. "And I didn't lie."

True. Every word was true.

Maia stared at the glowing stones in the dagger, betrayed, wondering if the damn thing even worked. But she said, gripping the edge of her composure by her fingernails, "If you don't tell me the truth, I'll kill you here and now."

The stones went dark. Dull.

Fuck.

Kheir's eyes marked the change in her, watching her unravel before his eyes, and he sighed sadly, leaning even heavily on the bars. "You want to know if what I said about your aunt trying to assassinate your parents is true."

Maia gave a clipped nod, clenching her jaw. She was falling to pieces and unsure how to stop it, how to put them back together when she was unmade.

This was the Sapphire Knight's fault—she blamed it all on Azrail. If it had only been Kheir's words, Maia could have shaken them off and moved on with her life, even if she'd never quite obey her aunt as faithfully. But with Azrail adding strength to Kheir's version of events ... she couldn't ignore that they both said the Sapphire Knight hadn't set those bombs to explode on Old Year's Night.

And if that was true ... all of it, every vicious thing he'd said could be the truth, too.

"Do you know of Wylnarren, and what happened to it?" Kheir asked, his eyes dull, as if he dove into his memories. As if he'd been there and seen it—or at least he'd beheld what remained of it. "You know that the traps around the city led to its demise?"

"Because its lord and lady failed to defend the city correctly," Maia agreed, her hands trembling and icy cold spreading through her hands. Her boots scraped the damp stone as she shuffled her weight, but she made herself still, forcing composure.

"Because there were too many Wylnarans, and their enemies were losing," Kheir corrected viciously. "Because they weren't under attack by a rebel militia like they believed, or even a militia funded by the Felis Empire like their generals suspected." True—all true, every word setting the Dagger of Truths glowing. "Their enemies played dirty. Your aunt backed the attackers in secret, sent soldiers to their frontlines disguised as civilians, and gave them a warehouse full of explosives and magic. Wylnarren didn't stand a chance."

True, all fucking true. This, at least, Maia could accept. "And why do you believe my aunt did it?" she asked carefully, her voice neutral through sheer will. A drop of freezing water slid through a crack in the ceiling and dropped down her spine, but she didn't even flinch, unnaturally still.

"Wylnarren is positioned in the center of the Sainsa Empire, with links to every other major city. Not a bad place to launch an invasion from."

Maia blinked. Choked on a laugh. But one look into his eyes and she saw he believed it.

She shook her head, her steps scraping the dirty floor as she stalked a few paces away, and didn't bother to look at the dagger—this was nothing but Kheir's opinion. "If my aunt wanted to conquer anywhere, why would she choose Sainsa? The Salt King's Sea separates us; it takes seven days to cross. It would make more sense to cross the Crooked Finger between us and Venhaus to our left, or march straight into Lower Aether."

Kheir laughed, a weak puff of sound. "Your aunt doesn't have a burning grudge against either of those empires. Besides, we all know Lower Aether's army is too impressive for her to risk, and the wild beastkind of Venhaus makes an invasion complicated. She wants her sister dead, princess. She wants your mother dead. And you know why."

Maia wanted to laugh; she knew nothing. Absolutely fucking *nothing*. She was kept so far in the dark, she'd made the Wolven Lord's chasm her home. But she held that crack of laughter inside, lifted her chin, and kept her cool. "That's where you're wrong."

Kheir measured her, pity in his eyes. Maia bared her teeth. "Ismene was in love with Kaladeir when she was young. Maybe she still is."

Maia straightened abruptly. Kaladeir. Her father. She blinked, blinked again, and laughed in disbelief. "You expect me to believe my aunt tried to assassinate her own sister, the queen of an empire we're allied with, over *a man?*"

"Never been in love, I take it, princess?" Kheir asked, his voice syrupy and slow and his copper wings fluttering slowly. "Love has launched more wars than hate, anger, and jealousy. More than all of them put together."

Maia stared, her heartbeat loud in her ears. "The Vassal Empire isn't at war."

"Then why," he asked, panting, "are armies being built in the mountain camps?"

"They're not." Maia frowned, staring at the dead stones in

the dagger at her words. "They're not," she repeated, her certainty starting to crumble. "Are they?"

"Yes," Kheir breathed, and the dagger glowed.

"Shit." Maia let that truth settle into her, cold spiking through her body. And if the prince was right about that, he was likely right about the assassination attempt. Saints, her aunt had levelled a city, and all because a man had married her sister instead. "Who?" she asked Kheir, her heart thumping her ribs. If the Vassal Empire went to war, the city she knew and loved so much would look vastly different. Likely, Vassalaer's gates would be locked shut to newcomers, the residents holed up inside barricaded homes, the library and museums and galleries converted into sick bays, and the workshops transformed into munitions factories. She'd read enough books on the history of the Saintslands; she knew how war would unfold. "Who are we at war with?"

"Right now?" Kheir replied weakly, pressing his wan gold face to the bars. "No one. But soon? My guess would be Sainsa."

Maia's ancestral home. Ismene's own sister's empire.

"And what about the Old Year's Night disaster?" she demanded, stepping closer, locking her body to stave off a shudder. Her fear made her colder than even the chill of these cells. "You said my aunt orchestrated that, too." She tried to scoff, to sound disbelieving, but her belief was crumbling to ashes. She hated it, and hated the way the loathing that already filled every corner and passage of her heart had spread, had swelled into something that would not stand her to remain in this palace for another day. Another minute.

But the consequences of running were as bad as those of regicide. *Queenkiller. Kinslayer.* She shook the words out of her head like batting annoying flies from her hair.

"She did," Kheir slurred, and Maia took a good look at him, really scanning him as he slumped fully against the bars.

Blood soaked down his right side, from a deep wound beneath his armpit, and Maia spat a vulgar word, breathless with sudden panic. For a reason she couldn't pinpoint the sight of his blood made a cold sweat break out down her spine, terror taking hold. A flash of deadly rage made her want to hunt down those who'd hurt him, so she could make them pay.

But she knew whose hand had done this, and there was no making *him* suffer—there was only enduring the suffering he put *her* through.

Maia stared at Kheir, sick with worry, and opened her lips to let out a deep hum. *Stay awake,* her song commanded, *don't you dare sleep.*

A plan was forming. Hasty and reckless, but ... her conscience wouldn't accept anything else. And *not* doing anything ... that was worse than any consequences she could think of. She'd rather face *him* than condone this. The glade of trees in her soul had withered to skeletal branches, her soul full of ashes. Kheir's words and the Dagger's truth stripped away any conviction she had holding her together, made her face who she really was—not just Ismene's weapon. She didn't know who she was without being the queen's tool, but she knew who she *wanted* to be, and that person wouldn't leave Kheir here to die.

No, she'd thought when Ismene told her to crush Kheir's mind, her entire soul wrenching away from the command. The word echoed through her now, as the prince slid down the dirty bars to the floor, letting out a grunt of pain. Shit. Maia could no longer breathe. Was he still alive?

She shoved past her shaky panic and put more force into her song, holding him this side of consciousness by sheer will. *Stay,* her song demanded, pleaded. *Stay with me.*

Kheir groaned, his mind welcoming her threads of power this time, as if he sensed what she offered. Maia's song hooked into his consciousness, and he rolled onto his back on the grimy, blood-streaked floor, his eyes staring up at the ceiling of the cell as he panted.

"I'll bleed out anyway," he pointed out.

Maia shut out the words.

Not if I have anything to say about it, she decided, and transformed her song into a simpler, louder melody, one that only she could hear. The notes glided through her body and entwined with the vital parts that kept her alive, wrapping around her muscles, around her bones, and settled in her arms—in her hands.

Not examining the vicious panic that fuelled her, she gripped two of the bars on his cell. She gritted her teeth, refusing to end her song even as she wrenched the two apart an inch, and then another, and another, and another until they were wide enough for a person to fit. She let her song fade, unsteady on her feet now, but she wasted no time in scrambling through the gap and into the cell, kneeling beside Kheir. It was a lot of blood. Too much. Her face burned, her stomach cramping—she was going to be sick. Or cry. Or both.

Kheir flinched away, but she hushed him, gently batting his hands aside as she pulled his tunic up to expose the wound in his side. It went all the way from front to back, she knew. Maia had a similar one on her thigh. "My healing isn't the most efficient magic," she said quietly, apologetically, and began to hum a slow, calming lullaby about star-filled skies and moonlit nights. It was enough to pull the wound together, to seal it, but she could do nothing about the blood loss. And he'd scar, she realised, tracing her finger over the thin white line. She had to clench her jaw against tears at the feel of him whole and healed, and didn't know why she was so affected. But it had been a rough day; she wasn't exactly emotionally balanced right now.

"Now it's my turn," Kheir panted, his chocolate eyes glassy but fixed on her as she kept tracing that scar, unable to draw back, "to ask you *why?*"

Maia met his hazy eyes, and didn't know the answer to that question. Not yet. "Because doing anything else is … unacceptable," she replied finally, and tore her fingers from his feverish skin with more effort than it should have taken. "Can you stand?"

"I doubt it," Kheir replied, some of the kindness she remembered re-entering his gaze. "But I'll try." He slid her a look, seeing right through to her soul again. Maia held his gaze, and wasn't afraid of what he saw. She was trying—to do better, to *be* better. "You don't happen to have some foolish notion of breaking me out, do you?"

Maia laughed, her lips curving and relief sagging her shoulders at the humour—the life—in his gleaming brown eyes. "Me? Never."

"It won't work," he said, his smile forgiving her of what she'd done to land him here. Maia's throat closed up; she stood in a rush, the leather of her dress creaking, and avoided his gaze as she slipped back through the gap in the bars. She didn't dare look at the occupants of the other cells around her. She would come back for them, she promised herself.

"It will," she disagreed. "And they'll never know it was me, or be able to track you down. It'll be fine."

Kheir gritted his teeth as he shoved off the floor, fingers sliding through his own blood. Maia took a step back towards the cell to help, but he got awkwardly to his feet and staggered out into the aisle with stubborn determination on his face. For someone pushing back against an escape attempt, he looked remarkably like a man escaping. She gave him a wry smile.

"It's a shame you work for Queen Ismene," Kheir said,

meeting her eyes with warmth that thawed her icy bones. "You and I could have been friends. Could have been more."

Maia glanced away, her chest tightening. Tears stung her eyes for no logical reason. "Yeah, well, let's not dwell on that, shall we?"

"You're not coming with me," he observed, taking a step after her, steady enough that she didn't throw her arm around his back no matter how hard an inner voice urged her to. "You'll stay and do her bidding."

Maia sighed, and met his eyes, giving him the only thing she could: the truth. "I don't see a way out for me. Not today and not ever." She'd never imagined freedom in her fantasies, only revenge and satisfaction before the Foxes and palace guard closed in around her, before the executioner's blade drove through the back of her neck. "But I'll get you out," she added, assessing his beaten face, his messy bronze hair and blood-stained ... well, everything. She opened her mouth and sang, a song she'd never used before but one that came easily, as if the saints themselves had given her it. Beside her, his clothes became clean but dull, homespun, and his features roughened, his hair a dirty blonde. Unrecognisable.

"I don't know how long it'll last," she said, as he glanced at his hands, no longer long-fingered and calloused, but rough and large. She shuddered hard, imagining how they'd feel against her body, wanting to compare with Kheir's real hands, wanting—just wanting. She was tired of wanting. It only got her hurt. "You'll have to be quick. Come on."

She kept an eye on him, half expecting his legs to give out again as she stalked up the aisle towards the steps, not daring to look into the cells full of people she was leaving behind in favour of this prince. Not because she valued them less, she promised herself—because she'd put Kheir here herself. Because it was her *fault*, and she needed to right a wrong.

Never mind that the trees at the bottom of her soul leant towards him like he was the sun.

"I didn't know you were telling the truth," she said quietly as they walked, Kheir with difficulty but fast enough to impress her.

"If you had, what difference would it have made?" he asked, his footsteps scraping, breathing laboured.

Maia mulled it over, looking hard at the truths she usually avoided. "I suppose we'd both be locked down here." They reached the staircase, the hardest part of their escape route for Kheir to tackle. She just hoped he wasn't too dizzy to scale the steps. "If anyone asks, I met you at Silvan's and brought you home for a fumble."

Kheir barked a sudden laugh that made her stomach erupt with butterflies. "Oh, that's my cover story, is it?"

She made to lean against the dark stone wall, but thought better of it at the slimy texture of its surface. "It's either that, or a servant boy."

His eyes, now a dull grey, slid to her with amusement. "You're not my usual type, princess. But I could make an exception for someone so gallant and heroic."

"Oh, you flatterer," Maia replied, keeping up a rapport as they began to climb the stairs. "But I can't blame you for being swayed by me." She batted her lashes. "I'm a rare, incredible specimen."

"Your ego is as big as the eastern star," he joked, and scaled four steps before he'd even noticed. Good.

Maia snorted. They could definitely have been friends —*very* good friends—under different circumstances. It was a shame that they'd had to meet like this. It burned in her chest, feeding her hate and anger.

"If you're ever in the north, come to V'haiv City," Kheir said, his hand pressed to the wall as he slowly ascended ahead of her. Maia kept a step behind him in case he slipped, every scuff of his feet making her tense in alarm. "Say you're a friend of mine."

The look he slid her way implied a double meaning: if she needed somewhere to hide, he offered his home. Maia just nodded, unable to think of a life outside Vassalaer. It was all she'd ever known, this city that owned her heart.

"Almost there," she said, praying her song held his illusion together. "When we reach the top, there's a gate to your right; go through it, and follow the path to its end. The road at the bottom will lead you straight to the Erythrun Bridge, and from there you'll see the southern gate out of the city."

"You make it sound so easy," Kheir said with a weak laugh, his leg faltering before he made the next step. "I might die before I ever make it to the gate."

"Oh, don't be so dramatic," Maia huffed, ignoring the way her sickness spiked. Her fault—if he did die, it would all on her head, the blood on her hands. And worse, she wanted him to live. She *liked* him. She'd hate herself if he died, would turn all the hatred festering in her soul for Ismene inward. "You'll be fine. It's hardly a ten minute walk, and then you're out."

"Hardly a ten minute walk," he repeated dubiously.

"There's the archway," Maia said with relief, humming under her breath, praying to the saints that the illusion around Kheir held out against the power on the dungeon exit.

"There's magic—" he began.

"I know," she snapped, and kept on humming, turning it into a sharper song, ruthless and forceful. Her hands shook as they neared, the exit seven steps away, then five, then three. She didn't dare hold her breath as Kheir stepped onto that last step, holding her song in her throat in a defiant note.

Her melody cut out as the magic barrier shoved Kheir back, the prince nearly toppling onto Maia and sending them both sprawling down the steps with a shriek. She managed to keep her balance, grappling desperately at the gaps between bricks in the walls, her fingernails breaking. The feeling of falling was jarring, but she steadied, breathing fast and gripping Kheir so hard that she'd be adding more bruises to his collection.

"I knew it," Kheir said quietly, miserably, shaking where his body pressed against hers. In the midst of panic, a sense of rightness hit, with a desperate urge to grab his face and kiss him senseless. But she fought it; now was *so* not the time.

Maia sucked in a breath, steadied Kheir on the step, and ripped a song from her throat to beat the dungeon shield into submission. She'd yet to meet something she couldn't crush with her power, had yet to find something she couldn't snare. She'd only failed with Kheir because of her aversion to killing him. If she'd been a hundred percent convicted, like she was now ... he wouldn't have stood a chance.

"Go!" Maia ordered as she felt the invisible wall buckle. Barely long enough for them to both scramble through, but it was long enough. "That way," she reminded him out in the fresh air, the gardens a snow-covered blur in front of her as she grabbed Kheir's shoulders and turned him. "Follow the path to its end."

"I remember," he replied, hesitating. He lifted a bloody hand, skimming Maia's cheek to push a lock of silver hair behind her ear. "Saints watch over you," he said in farewell.

"And you," she replied, her throat burning as he walked away. She turned in place, scanning the snaking garden path around them for palace guards. The cry of a wood pigeon made her jump, but she didn't spy any uniforms or swords.

"Leovan's hairy cock," she swore viciously, and hoped the saint of love would forgive her for the curse as she spotted not guards but *Naemi* hurrying towards her, a look of disapproval and worry on her friend's face.

CHAPTER FIFTEEN

"I've been looking for you everywhere," Naemi breathed in relief, her amber eyes gentle as they met Maia's—before her attention snagged on Kheir's retreating form. He'd hidden his wings, thank fuck. With them on display, he'd never blend into the Vassalians. "Who was that?"

Maia sighed heavily, amping up the drama even as her heart beat thrice as fast as was healthy. "Remember when I went to Silvan's without you last week, and I met that guy?"

"That's *him*?" Naemi watched Kheir's retreating back as he sped up, closing the gate behind him and wasting no time in descending the steep path. Maia's heart crumpled. Lying to her friend coated her tongue with a sickly taste. She could have told Naemi, but she wouldn't draw her best friend into this—she'd only get Naemi punished, too. "He's taller than I imagined. Bigger, too."

"Bigger where it counts," Maia joked, but Naemi didn't laugh. Her eyes had drawn to the doorway to the dungeons, still cracked open. Maia was going to be sick.

"Why meet him here?" Naemi asked. Her voice was

curious—she didn't realise what Maia had done, thank the saints.

"Nobody ever comes out here," Maia replied with a flippant shrug and a crooked grin. "It's a bit bleak, but it's the only place I can find privacy with all the guards and staff around. Not to mention the courtiers."

Naemi knew she was lying; Maia could see it in the tightening lines around her eyes, the smile that turned from easy to strained. It was the Dagger of Truths that sealed her fate. Maia had forgotten she was holding it.

"Where did you get that?"

Maia swallowed, scrambling for a flippant response. Her soul shrivelled, her gut clenching. She had nothing.

"Maia," Naemi sighed, her amber eyes bleak. That was disappointment in her voice—and a lack of surprise, as if she'd been waiting for Maia to slip up and break the rules. "Oh, Maia, what have you done?"

Maia swallowed, scanning her friend's round, golden face and seeing nothing but that hateful disappointment. "The right thing," she said finally, faintly. She whispered, "The only thing I could live with."

"Who was that man?" Naemi pressed, looking to the gate. Gone—Kheir was gone. That was good. Maia could buy him enough time to get out of the city, if she could do nothing else. If she couldn't keep the blade from swinging down to her own neck. "Who did you let him visit?"

Visit?

Maia didn't let her hope show. Naemi thought she'd snuck him *into* the dungeons, not snuck him out.

"My aunt tried to kill my parents," she blurted, searching for *anything* to stall Naemi before she shouted for the guards, or whatever else she'd do when she realised what Maia had really done. She knew Naemi would never do anything to hurt *her*, but Naemi had no loyalty to Kheir. "This is the

Dagger of Truths, Naemi." She lifted it, smoky brown stones glowing, as if encouraging Maia. "There's no way for anyone to deceive me when I have this, and the prisoner, the prince, told the truth. Ismene tried to kill my parents."

The truth cut the air like a scythe.

Naemi's nostrils flared slightly, something in her beautiful face shifting. Maia's stomach twisted sickly even though she didn't understand why. "You don't know anything, Maia," Naemi breathed, her gentle voice edged with steel. A feather sharp enough to slice skin, as dangerous as any blade. "What the queen does, she does for very good reasons."

Maia blinked.

Blinked again.

Everything in her had gone horribly still, surprise making her a statue. Not even the fat bees buzzing in the gardens, or the birds swooping down for food could unfreeze her.

"Are you saying it's not true," she asked slowly—so slowly, "or are you saying it *is* true, and you're perfectly okay with my aunt trying to kill my parents?" It came out calm, *too* calm considering the crash and flare of emotions inside her. The trees of her soul thrashed in the wake of a powerful storm.

"Maia, you don't know anything about your parents," Naemi said softly, her amber eyes large and beseeching as she reached out to clasp Maia's hand. Maia moved out of reach, her fingers tightening on the Dagger of Truths. "You *know* Queen Ismene; you know you can trust her. She always does what's right for the Vassal Empire."

Except Maia had never been able to trust Ismene. She'd always obeyed her, always respected and feared her, but trusted her? No. Not since that day Maia had refused to use her power. Not since the darkness and terror and pain that came as punishment. Naemi would never understand that, would she? She'd never once said no, had never suffered the consequences.

Had she ever *wanted* to refuse? Maia had always thought Naemi endured the court and crown, the same as *she* did, but maybe ... maybe Naemi had always fit in better than Maia had. Maybe Maia had seen kinship because she'd been looking for it.

"Was *this* right?" Maia asked, her voice tight. Her stillness broke as she reached for the grime-stained hem of her red dress and didn't give a *shit* that she was baring more skin than she'd like as she lifted the fabric to show the white slice across her thigh, hauling it higher to reveal the biggest, most gruesome scar across her stomach. "Was *this* for the good of the Vassal Empire?"

"Princess," Naemi sighed sadly, reaching to grasp her hand. Maia let her dress fall and moved another step back. "You don't know what it takes to rule an empire," Naemi said in that kind voice, patiently waiting for Maia to see sense.

"And you do?" Maia shot back, starting to shake. Naemi had looked at her scars and seen a reasonable punishment. Maia had been *thirteen*. Her fae healing had erased all the smaller scars—and there'd been many—but the ones she'd been left with ... vicious. Vile. Wounds so bad that even her advanced healing had struggled to close them. And Naemi had practically shrugged. "Since when do you run an empire, Naemi?"

Naemi put a hand on her heart over her dress, imploring Maia to listen. This was the friend she'd known for years, but Maia no longer recognised her. Couldn't stand to look her in the eye. "I'm her lady in waiting; I'm privy to things you'll never know. And that's *okay*, you don't *need* to know them—"

"Yeah, that's enough of that," Maia cut off, turning away and taking a random path into the gardens, *anything* to get away from her friend. The friend who looked at her scars and saw a reasonable way to treat a thirteen year old, who told Maia *to her face* that her parents' murders would have been good for this empire.

"Princess," Naemi called, hurrying after her. Maia didn't expect her to catch up; Maia had always been swifter, stronger. It was about the only good thing her aunt had done for her—given her training. "Maia!"

She'd never expected to hear this horseshit from her best friend, never expected such lack of care in her face, especially at the marks of the worst pain Maia had ever suffered.

Why was she so loyal to Ismene? Maia had colossally miscalculated, had thought Naemi was her best friend so would be most loyal to *her*, but ... she was the queen's lady through and through.

I'm her lady in waiting; I'm privy to things you'll never know. And that's okay, you don't need to know them—

The words cut into her heart like barbs, festered in her mind like poison. Maia took turn after turn through the hedges and flower trails, hardly even seeing the living arches she walked through, the fountains she raced past. The sounds of trickling water and birds chirping *barely* filtered through the noise in her mind. If Naemi was still calling her name, she couldn't hear her.

Finally, she lost Naemi among the rose bushes and lily ponds, not seeing the greenery and colours spinning around her. Her twisting path only exacerbated the merry-go-round of her thoughts. She dragged sharp breaths into her lungs, honeysuckle and gardenia coating her tongue like delicate poison.

She felt ... betrayed. That was the only word for the feeling corroding her insides, making her emotions brittle and her bottom lip tremble wildly. She'd thought Naemi would always back her up, even factoring in Maia skirting the edge of treason. She'd thought Naemi would *always* be on her side, no matter what life threw at them.

Even in those murderous fantasies, Maia had never dreaded Naemi turning on her, had only feared the palace guard. Naemi would never do something like that—she was *Naemi*. But maybe Maia had loved Naemi more than *she'd* ever loved Maia; maybe she'd been Maia's best friend, but Maia had been a friend, plain and simple. A worse thought crept up like an assassin in the night: maybe she'd only been friends with her because Ismene had asked her to. Was Maia's entire friendship a command?

The gardens blurred as Maia shoved past citrus-bearing hedges and elegant, flowering trees, her shoes trampling the fluffy grass underfoot. She was deep in the gardens now, but she didn't care, might never leave them.

She questioned *everything*. Every time Naemi had laughed at one of Maia's jokes, had it been forced? Every night out—had that been her *job*, to accompany Maia, to keep her in check so she didn't embarrass the crown too badly? Every hug and smile and shared lightning biscuit … was every moment a fabrication?

Maia marched around a row of orange trees—and slammed into a solid body. She reared back, blinking hard to clear her tear-slick eyes. For a second, dizzy with heartache and betrayal, she expected to look up into the Sapphire Knight's tanned, handsome face. Instead, it was a face that made her blood run cold.

He was pale, icy-haired, and strikingly elegant, the sort of man you looked at twice, but the utter lack of humanity or feeling in his hazel eyes warned you to stay far, *far* away. He was ten years older than Maia, and had used every moment of that extra time on the earth to hone his cruelty to a degree that had never been seen before. Or since.

"Your aunt's looking for you," Etziel said mildly, putting a hand on Maia's shoulder and steering her away from where she'd been heading. Her skin crawled where his hand rested, and her heart beat like a panicked rabbit, thumping her ribcage, trying to escape, to *flee*. "She seems worried about you, princess," he went on, as if this was ordinary, as if they were *friends*. As if he hadn't carved her up until she screamed.

"I thought you were in Thelleus," she breathed, ducking out from under his hold and walking a step behind him, *refusing* to put him at her back. Her whole body vibrated with awareness and threat, her chest painfully tight. Escape —she had to escape. But there were two ways this would play out; Maia could protect herself and play along, or run and make herself his prey.

"I *was* in Thelleus," Etziel agreed cordially, linking his hands behind himself as he strolled through the gardens, the picture of courtly grace in his pale blue jacket and trousers. But she could smell the iron and blood on him, no matter how saintly he looked, he was—and always would be—a monster. "But I'm here to oversee some business, at our queen's behest. This way."

Maia almost followed him, almost fell back on her old habits of doing what she was told in a panicked bid to avoid consequences, but ... with Etziel here, with her shoulder still burning where he'd touched her... *No*. Not in a thousand ages would she follow him anywhere.

It wasn't smart, and she knew how it would end, but Maia twisted off the path and leapt over a low hedge. As she landed heavily on the other side, she sent a growl of power off her tongue, a song or melody beyond her fear-addled mind.

It landed messily, making Etziel trip over his own feet, but not knocking him onto his ass the way she'd intended as she threw herself through the rows of fruit trees. Shit, he was going to catch her. He was the queen's best hunter after all, her favourite assassin.

Maia needed to think clearly, to sing a complex song, but

her throat had closed up, and every memory of those long days he'd tormented her replayed, wrapping around her neck like a noose. A traitor—she was a traitor to the crown for freeing Kheir, and Etziel had been brought here to torture her again.

It didn't matter that there hadn't been nearly enough time between her letting Kheir out and Etziel arriving to allow the two-day journey from Thelleus. Her terrified mind told her he had come for her, and she would die—but not before he wrought so many screams from her throat that skin tore and her voice broke. Maybe this time her voice would give out for good, and she'd never regain the ability to speak.

"Why do you run, princess?" Etziel called, close behind her as she leapt over rose bushes and swung around pear trees. Too close. She'd never found out what power Etziel had, if he had any at all, but she was surely in range of it now. Maia tried to sing a shield around herself, to make her skin impenetrable as steel, but she could barely gasp out a note, the gardens spinning around her. Lack of air, she knew, but could do nothing about it. "Her Majesty just wants a word," Etziel went on, loud enough to make every cell in her body scream at his nearness—and then there was a fist clutching her hair, wrenching her back, and agony roared through her skull as strands ripped out. "Running makes you look guilty, but you don't have anything to confess to, do you princess?"

Maia shook her head, her chest a mess of pain and panic. She couldn't breathe, couldn't think, couldn't stop shaking. Overhead a lone gull paused to observe them, but no bird could save Maia now. Nothing could.

She plummeted rapidly into her self-preservation instincts: obey, be silent, give them whatever they asked for without even a blink of defiance.

"Who do you think set the shields around the dungeons, Maia?" Etziel asked, his tone of voice too normal as he yanked her body back against him. "She knows you went to visit the prince."

But not about Kheir's escape? Maia's chest hitched, a breath of relief trying and failing to form.

"I think she'll let me loose on you again, don't you?" Etziel asked, a smile in his disgustingly civil voice. He turned her around to face his hateful, beautiful face and let go of her hair, smoothing the silver strands back into place. "You're not going to run again, are you, Maia?"

She shook her head fast, tears of pain burning hot paths down her cheeks. It would happen again—every bit of torment, every nightmare that still sent her lurching awake in the middle of the night nine years later. Etziel's smile softened, real warmth in it as he brushed her cheek. He didn't seem to notice that she shook so hard that her teeth rattled.

"Come on, let's not keep the queen waiting."

It was sheer luck that kept the Dagger of Truths concealed in her skirts, or maybe some saint's hand turning his gaze away from Maia's right hand.

Maia was paralysed as Etziel took her hand, his smile still in place as he tugged her down the garden path on uncooperative feet. Frozen with obedience, Maia followed, and wondered if Naemi would say this was for the good of the Vassal Empire, too: this hand her attacker had coiled like a deadly snake around her own, ready to strike and fill her with unbearable venom until she blacked out.

CHAPTER SIXTEEN

Kheir Rizian was going to pass out. He knew it, and could do nothing to stop it as he followed the princess's instructions, hugging the palace walls as he stumbled as fast as he could down the path, flinching at every distant shout and rattling carriage. Blood crusted his tunic beneath his arm and all down his right side, a gift from a cruel guard that had ultimately failed to get what he wanted: Kheir's acquiescence to Queen Ismene's plans to expand the slave caravans.

Why she wanted it so badly, and why she needed V'haiv's permission, Kheir couldn't imagine.

What he *did* know was that she'd never get it from him, and certainly not from his parents. He'd been sent on this diplomatic mission to achieve the *opposite*, to establish an alliance and dismantle the caravans if possible, or reduce them if Ismene wouldn't budge on their existence. This was their first method: diplomacy and negotiation. Their next step wouldn't be quite so polite, and would involve deploying the deadliest, swiftest, and cleverest soldiers in their armies to stop the caravans ever reaching their destinations. Wherever that actually was—none of his parents' best spies had been able to find out.

But he shouldn't have been worrying about that now; he should have been focused on the itchy feeling of Maia's magic wearing off and the weakness seeping back into his body, the blood seeping *out* with every step down the steep path to the city proper.

He made it to the street at the bottom through sheer stubbornness, pausing to drag in three panting breaths as he scanned the street for the guards people called Foxes, checking for their burnt orange uniforms in shop porches, or weaving among the clusters of people browsing the boutiques that lined the street, or patrolling down the broad avenue to his left. He spotted one of them standing outside the imposing council building down the street, but as long as Kheir kept his wound hidden and stayed on the other side of the road, the crowd should carry him along. And of course, as long as he didn't faint in the middle of the road. At least the sweet, perfumed air coming from a fragrance shop a few paces down would mask the scent of his blood. Saints knew that coppery tang was all *he* could smell, not helping his lightheadedness at all.

Kheir drew another breath, wishing like hell that he wasn't alone, wishing his mum and dad and sisters were here, even across the city waiting for him. Fuck, he'd even take them being across this saintsforsaken empire—rather than across the sea and the continent, *months* away. But he had nobody to encourage him, to give him strength as he struggled down the road, focussing hard on not missing a step. Pain raging through his body, but he gritted his teeth as his vision wavered and struggled on. Oddly, it was Maia's face that stuck with him, that kept him putting one foot in front of the other no matter how much it hurt.

He passed the council building, passed the boutiques

selling delicate, sculpted cakes, beaded dresses worth a king's ransom, and furniture carved with intricate scenes of the saints, and by the time the awe-inspiring, elaborate shop fronts had changed to stately terrace houses—likely belonging to minor councillors—Kheir could smell the river's citrusy musk, could glimpse the white stone arch of the Erythrun Bridge Maia had told him to cross.

"Thank the saints," he gasped under his breath, the barbers he passed blurring into streaks of colour and light like magic, the people he passed nothing more than formless, unknowable monsters.

The street became a whirlwind around him as dizziness took firm hold, and Maia's face crossed his mind again as he was forced to stop to let a cart and procession of horses go clattering past. She was stunning in the same way the stars were beautiful—distant, cold, and mysterious. But there was so much pain within her, so much anger and hate that it bled through her icy mask. And when she'd helped him escape, that bright, smiling person she'd unveiled like the petals of a night-blooming flower ... he'd listed towards her, as if she sang a siren song to his soul.

The cart rolled on, the road clear. It seemed an insurmountable distance to cross now he'd stopped moving, but he had to keep going. If only so Maia's sacrifice hadn't been in vain. She would be punished, he knew. Kheir wouldn't squander the gift of freedom she'd given him.

Almost there, he told himself as he staggered across the road to the bridge, wishing his mother was here to say the words, to hold his hand. Saints, he was a baby for wanting his mum right now, but he did. He wanted her so badly, and he didn't think he was going to make it across the bridge and out of the city. He didn't think he'd ever make it back to V'haiv City, ever see those copper domes and verdigris towers ever again. He'd never hear the twang of his father's music or his sisters' chorus of laughter, would never smell honey and spices—home. He focused on those memories, holding them close as he stumbled down the endless bridge.

"Indira," he rasped as he made his shaky way across the pale, arched stones, invoking the Healer, saint of rest and recovery. "I need your help."

He didn't expect an answer; the saints weren't active in their assistance after all, but they watched from afar. He wasn't surprised when he didn't get a reply.

"Watch it," a woman snapped when Kheir tumbled off the other end of the bridge, miraculously making it across to a road surrounded by tall grey-brick buildings and fragrant trees. He just managed to twist himself away so he didn't fall on the dark-haired woman glaring at him. Instead, he slammed into the merciless ground, the impact jolting every pain in his body into agony until he choked on a sound of pain.

"Ev, be kind," a soft male voice chided. "Are you alright?"

It took Kheir a moment to realise the man was talking to him, but by this point, speech was beyond him. He only groaned, and inhaled sharply as a man with red hair threaded with luminous purple knelt in front of him, his features sharp and elegant. Fae, he thought, like himself, but he didn't see pointed ears. The man reached for him to help him back to his feet, accidentally brushing Kheir's injured side, and he bit down on a scream, muffling it.

"Fuck," the man breathed, paling beneath his freckles—noticing the blood, smelling it probably. "You need help."

Kheir laughed, a sharp burst of sound. He knew damn well he needed help, but he had no safe place to seek it. "I need ... the gate."

He gestured uselessly at the vast gate to their right, where Maia had told him to go. He knew he'd never make it in this pitiful state. He'd barely made it across the bridge—the gate was six times that distance.

The man's jade green eyes flicked from the gate back to him and narrowed in understanding. But how *could* he understand? Had word spread of Kheir's escape so soon? His stomach whirled like a storm, cramping hard. The guards would already be scouring the streets for him. He'd be lucky to survive to nightfall; if his injuries didn't kill him, Ismene would.

"It's alright," the man soothed, blocking out the bright glare of the sun as he leaned closer. "There's somewhere we can take you, a safe place. But it's too far for you to go when you're hurt."

"There's a Hall of Indira not too far from here," the woman Kheir had almost knocked down said, sounding surly about the offer. "Come on, get up, we'll take you there."

"Thank you," Kheir rasped as she reached for him, her hands surprisingly gentle given her prickly countenance. They were careful of his injury, but she didn't know about the bruises and cuts covering the rest of him courtesy of the queen's hunter. She accidentally pressed on a cut that sent pain tearing right to Kheir's side, somehow inflaming the bloody injury into an unbearable torture. The world went black in an instant.

※

When Kheir woke, his arms were flat at his sides in an unnatural position, and clean-smelling white sheets had been tucked suffocatingly tight around his chest. He might as well have been dressed for a coffin; he expected the wooden walls to be nailed shut around him at any moment. But when he cracked his sore eyes open, he found a bright, high-ceilinged hall with light slanting through tall windows and a row of beds stretching out on either side of him, only one other bed occupied. The whole place smelled like herbs and astringent —like healing—and it was as quiet as a morgue, at least until clothes shuffled to his right.

"It's alright," a soft voice said, drawing his eye to the wooden chair beside his bed and the striking man who reclined in it. Tall and slim, with an elfin, beautiful face and eyes such a rare shade of jade that Kheir had never seen any like them before. Red-purple hair spilled over the shoulder of his pale grey shirt, and leather-clad legs stretched out in front of him, the buckles on his boots suggesting they were expensive. For a moment, Kheir just stared.

"You ... are uncommonly beautiful," was all he could think to say.

A smile split the man's face, making him even more stunning—painfully so. "You're pretty handsome yourself." But his smile slipped, worry shadowing his fine features. "Minus all the blood and grime. What happened?"

Kheir couldn't tell this beautiful stranger the truth. Not when the palace guard and the Foxes were surely searching for him by now, combing every street. It was a saint's blessing that none had checked this place.

"I was attacked," he said, drawing on his skills as a courtier to lie smoothly.

His rescuer's smile turned wry, jade eyes glittering as he leaned forward in his chair. "Attacked, and bleeding, and running for the city gate at the same time an enemy to the crown escaped the palace dungeons. Strange, that."

The blood drained from Kheir's face.

"I thought you were beastkind," the beautiful man said, batting a strand of red hair from his face as he leant even closer, all but hanging off the chair as he watched Kheir intently. "We've been going missing for weeks, and the disappearances are getting worse. I thought someone had tried to take you, and you'd fought back. But then the alarms were raised, and the Foxes were on every damn street corner, demanding to know if anyone had seen a V'haivan man with copper wings, brown hair, and dark eyes. Rumours spread," he added with a shrug. "And then the truth spread, among certain circles. Why are you an enemy to the crown?"

Kheir found he had no words. He only swallowed, and shook his head, a measly attempt at denial.

"I'll go first," the man said with a smile meant to set Kheir at ease, watching with something close to curiosity, edged with understanding. "I'm Jaromir Sintali, but my friends call me Jaro. When I was discovered seven years ago, I was indentured and assigned to work at the pillow rooms in the southside, in the palace quarter specifically. The lords and ladies like my delicate looks, or so I'm told," he added, smiling even as Kheir's face fell, his heart turning to stone. It was a barbaric act, indenturing anyone, let alone forcing them to work in *brothels*. No consent—there could never be any consent there.

He reached for Jaromir's hand without even thinking, without considering that he might not want the touch of a stranger, might be half sick of strangers touching him. "I'm sorry," Kheir said quietly, seriously. "It is not that way in V'haiv."

"No, there you just hunted us all down and killed us," Jaro replied, his words sharp but voice soft, as if he never raised it, as if he'd been ... trained to be that soft. Kheir removed his touch, but couldn't help himself and squeezed Jaro's hand before he made himself let go.

"We did," he agreed, not hiding from that sickening past. He'd be a coward and a shamefully bad prince if he refused to look V'haiv's dark, ugly past in its eye. There could be no fixing those errors, no doing better for future generations, if he was willfully half-blind. "But no beastkind have been hunted in eighty three years, and *many* have been born, families have grown—and they now live peacefully. My dearest friend is beastkind," he said, his heart hurting with longing. "She's a winter fox."

Jaromir's expression didn't change, but some of the tension left his eyes. "When I was indentured," he went on, "my younger brother was separated from me. I don't know where he was sent, only that he was taken out of the city, and no record has been found of him in seven years. He was twelve then, nineteen now."

Kheir's heart squeezed tight. He'd always been too soft, too sympathetic, but his parents had made him see it as strength, not weakness. That gentle heart would make him more than a good king, they told him—it would make him a *great* king.

"That's why *I'm* an enemy to the crown; because they took my brother from me, and sent him chasm knows where, without me."

Kheir watched Jaro's face, noting the tiny shifts of feeling behind the mask of softness and civility. "Not for what they've done to you?" he asked with a frown.

Jaro shook his head, sighing and sitting back in his chair. "That's all secondary."

It shouldn't be, Kheir nearly said, but it wasn't his place. So instead he said, "My name is Crown Prince Kheir Sin Rizian. I came here—"

"Your middle name is Sin?" Jaro blurted, his eyes crinkled as if he couldn't hold back that tiny hint of laughter. Kheir bet, with his masks removed, that laugh would be raucous. Loud enough to shake the saints' world.

"A warning and a promise," Kheir replied, giving Jaro a rakish grin. "In V'haivan it means shield."

Jaromir's lips twitched, his eyes alive for the first time. "Continue with your story."

Kheir took a slow breath. "I came here to present an alliance to Queen Ismene. She didn't agree with my plans, or my morals, and when I disagreed to back her plans to increase the slave caravans, she had her—she had someone try to control me, to manipulate me into agreeing."

Jaro reared back, pulling on the ends of his sleeves in a nervous gesture. "*Control* you? How?"

Kheir didn't want to say too much, but he sighed, and gave as much truth as he dared. "The woman who controlled me did so against her better judgement, and had as much choice in the matter as I was given. She was the one who helped me escape. Well ... that implies I was any use at all in the venture, which I was *not*. I'm here, as free as I might be, because of her. I'd rather not tell you her secrets."

Jaromir tilted his head, watching, weighing. The sun caught glimmers of pure ruby and amethyst in his hair, and Kheir found himself staring. He finally nodded. "I know who you mean. I've heard stories of the princess."

Kheir glanced away. He'd betrayed her, no matter how careful he'd tried to be. He expelled a breath through gritted teeth, his honour like a dented shield. "She's at risk. She set me free, and there can be no doubt that her aunt will punish her for it, if not kill her." Although Kheir's tactical mind told him Ismene wouldn't dispose of her most valuable asset. What she'd put Maia through instead ... it would be worse than death, perhaps.

If she allowed the bastard who'd tortured Kheir to touch Maia... Fierce, burning rage caught in his chest, not a wildfire but a chilling darkness, the blackness of a starless night.

Jaro dragged a hand through his hair, tugging on the roots slightly. "There's nothing we can do for her. If she were a regular traitor, maybe, but the *princess...*"

"I know," Kheir agreed, testing his body as he swung his

legs off the bed. He felt steady, if not completely pain free. "Thank you for helping me."

"Ev did most of the work. You might remember her as the woman who growled at you after you walked into her."

Kheir laughed softly, remembering bared teeth, heavy boots, and a dark braid. "I do indeed."

"She's a good healer and an even better person. She's just surly. Here, let me help you," Jaro offered, jumping out of his seat and supporting Kheir's back as he took an unsteady step.

"Why are you still here?" Kheir asked, and then winced. "I didn't mean that to sound so rude."

Jaro's mouth twitched, his eyes wry. "I don't mind rudeness. I'm used to it, with my friends. As for why I'm here... " He sighed, casting a glance around the hall. "Like I said, I thought you were beastkind at first, which makes you one of my very extended family." He laughed faintly, and Kheir smiled at the whispering sound. "And then I stayed out of curiosity, and because *someone* had to keep an eye on you. It's not a good idea to use the gates out of the city right now; they're being watched. I've got somewhere you can stay, though."

"Not here?" Kheir asked, looking around at the hall as he took another, steadier step. Strange—off balance without the weight of his wings. But it was safer to keep them hidden for now. He hoped the rest of the emissaries had left the palace, were safe somewhere, but judging by how swayed Valleir had been, that was a slim hope.

"No, that's not how our halls work," Jaro explained, supporting him for another step. "We come here for as long as it takes us to heal and then move on. It's a hospital more than anything." Jaro squeezed Kheir's arm.

The notion of it was confusing for Kheir, whose home had halls of Indira that welcomed people to stay for weeks, if not months. But as long as he had somewhere safe to lay low, that was all that mattered. "What do I owe you?" he asked. "For the help."

Jaro frowned deeply, a flicker of offence in his gaze before he masked it. "Nothing." He shook his head, his grip easy and careful as he helped Kheir cross the stone floor. "I know the Vassal Empire has a bad reputation, but we're not all unfeeling. And besides," he added with a sudden smile, "looking at your handsome face is payment enough."

Kheir barked a laugh, surprised and charmed. "Well, that's a lie if I've ever heard one. Where's this place you have for me? I should be able to make it there by myself."

Jaro snorted. "Not in the Wolven Lord's dark chasm. They're looking for a man on his own, not two people. I'm coming with you."

"You're very insistent," Kheir said, his mouth curving at the corners, warmth filling his chest. "But you're right. I'd be safer with you. And no matter what you say, I *do* owe you, and I'll find a way to repay you."

Jaromir rolled his eyes. "I told you, you owe me nothing. I'm used to picking up waifs and strays; you're no different, crown prince or not."

Kheir liked that, a great deal. "Then lead the way, Jaromir."

Kheir would hide out in this place Jaro had for him, and think of a way to save Maia before her aunt could do grievous damage. However difficult, he couldn't just leave Maia to her fate. She'd risked everything to get him out of that cell, and she'd been … kind and funny. There was a beautiful soul withering under all the darkness the court and crown suffocated her in, and Kheir would be damned if he left her there.

CHAPTER SEVENTEEN

Run, Maia screamed at herself, as if her consciousness was locked away in a deep chamber of her own self by some wicked form of magic. But there was no magic at play here, only the power called fear. It was every bit as effective as a curse, keeping her shaking and weak as Etziel led her back into the gleaming palace and through the bright, golden halls to her aunt's personal sitting room. Maia passed the marble drakes on the grand staircase and sent a pleading glance their way, as if they'd leap to life and defend her. But no one was coming to her rescue, not even her best friend. Maia was trapped —doomed.

Even knowing she was about to be named a traitor the second her aunt heard that Kheir had escaped, Maia couldn't get her trembling body to fight, couldn't get her shell of a body to do anything but follow Etziel's guiding push towards her aunt's private rooms. Memories played on a loop, her own screams echoing in her ears, and her hand shook so hard in Etziel's grip that the red beads dangling from her belt clacked together in a desperate percussion.

She met the eyes of every guard she passed, but they were loyal to Ismene, every one of them unfaltering. They didn't even meet her eyes as she was led, clearly terrified, shaking like a leaf in a storm, past them and into the warm, cloyingly sweet room where Ismene waited. There were no guards lurking by the curtained windows, no ladies in waiting on the emerald sofas, but Maia didn't let relief weaken her. Ismene probably didn't want an audience for this.

Ismene glanced up from her spot on the biggest sofa, took one look at Maia and sighed, directing her irritated gaze to Etziel. "What did you do to her? She looks halfway to death."

"Nothing, your Majesty," Etziel replied, letting go of Maia to bow deeply. Graceful and unthreatening. He was a better liar than even Maia. "I only escorted her here as you asked."

Ismene's lips thinned, but she nodded, golden hair swaying where it was pinned into a swirling updo to compliment the clouds on her dress. "You frighten her to death."

And whose fault was that? Maia wanted to scream. *Who let him loose upon me for my disobedience?* Etziel hadn't done it of his own volition, no matter how much he'd relished it. *She'd* given the order, or the permission—Maia had never been sure which it was, never knew if Etziel had been watching her before that day, imagining how she'd scream when he cut her.

She wanted, very suddenly, to be anywhere else. At the Library of Vennh, at Silvan's music hall, on the bridge over the Luvasa with the statues of the saints watching her with uncaring eyes. She'd settle for being in a gutter behind The Baton and Paintbrush if it meant escaping Etziel. She'd always been scared of her aunt for the power she wielded, for the single word it would take to condemn Maia, to send her back to Etziel's waiting tools—but she'd always been more scared of *him*, the one who'd done the bloody deeds.

"Leave us," Ismene sighed, giving Etziel a look that

expressed her displeasure. Or maybe it was irritation. No sympathy shone for Maia in her turquoise eyes when the queen faced her, no understanding on her magically smooth, beautiful face, only a scrutinising stare that pierced her down to the bone. Exactly what Maia had come to expect from her aunt. "Would you like to explain, niece, why you made a visit to my dungeons?"

Maia couldn't get her jaw to unlock. Her heart was beating so hard she was sure it would give out any second now. Her beads kept rattling as she shook, her teeth chattering a counter beat.

"Sit," Ismene ordered, leaning back against the embroidered back of the sofa with an expectant look.

But Maia knew if she took a single step, her legs would give out, so she stayed rooted to the spot.

"I," Maia rasped, unlocking her jaw with effort. Her voice was small, a powerless wisp. Her mind raced for an explanation. "I wanted to know w-why he lied," she said, struggling to form the words.

Ismene watched her for a long second, the penetrating stare of a snake. No matter how beautiful and regal she was, her venom shone through. "And?"

Maia scrambled for words, dragging sickly sweet air in through her nose. "He's intimidated by us."

Ismene's eyebrows flicked up in agreement. "As he should be. Why do you allow Etziel to scare you so?"

Maia shook her head, goosebumps flashing down her arms. There was no controlling something as vast and monstrous as this fear.

"I won't let him near you again," Ismene offered, and a knot loosened in Maia's chest until she added, "unless you give me a reason to." Ismene smiled, as if this was a blessing and not a threat, as if Maia would ever be able to sleep again.

The smile slid off Ismene's face when she scanned Maia

again, when she noticed the fists Maia had curled in her skirts, the fabric *barely* hiding the handle of the Dagger of Truths. "Show me your hands."

Maia's heart rattled in her chest, her body resuming its violent shaking. Dead—she was dead. She was going to bleed out here on this pretty carpet. That would be better than what Etziel planned, at least. She couldn't show her hand—and couldn't flee for the door. Both would show her guilt.

"Show me your hands, Maia," Ismene repeated, rising from the sofa, every inch the queen as she dominated even this informal space.

Maia took a step back, but she could find no other way out. She had to lie about why she had the dagger, had to think on her feet, spin a tale that even Ismene would believe.

Her fist shaking, Maia lifted her hand. Her breath hitched at her aunt's confusion, and then cut out entirely at the rage that followed, twisting the queen's face into something unattractive and pinched.

"What did he tell you?" Ismene asked calmly—that too-calm tone Maia had learned from her.

She meant to lie. Meant to tell the best story she could think of. But she was too afraid—and too angry. This woman had taken Maia in and then tried to kill her parents.

"Truths," Maia choked out finally, sweat trickling down her spine beneath her leather bodice.

If the glade in the center of her soul had been skeletal and bare before, now it curved inward, branches locking, protecting itself.

"*Which* truths?" Ismene demanded, surging forward in a rustle of skirts until she was three feet from Maia, her eyes on the blade, on the gems in its hilt. She didn't look like a beautiful queen now; she looked exactly like what she was. A monster.

"You tried to kill my parents," Maia gasped out, regaining

her voice—barely—at the cost of her safety. She should have stopped talking, should have shut up and never spoken again. It would have been safer, *so much* safer. But those were lies she desperately told herself, and she knew, looking her aunt in the eye, that there'd be no safety ever again. Maia would rot down in the dungeons, likely in Kheir's vacated cell. Or would she be put to the chopping block instantly?

No, Maia knew her aunt. She wouldn't make it quick; she'd give Maia to Etziel again, and only kill her when she finally broke.

Ismene rolled her eyes at the accusation, and denied nothing.

Maia inhaled sharply, her head pounding, her heart throwing itself frantically against the bars of its cage. "You—you hurt your own people. You killed *Liann*, your own daughter. The Old Year's Night tragedy was *your* doing."

Ismene sighed this time, pursing her lips at Maia as she cast a glance around the opulent emerald room. The same room Maia had tried to snare Kheir in. "I wouldn't expect you to understand a queen's reasons," she said, echoing what Naemi had said. The words struck like arrows. "Rebellion was growing, and that rebellion would have become a civil war in Vassalaer. More people than seventy-two would have died. I prevented that. And stamped out any trust in that vigilante while I was at it."

The Sapphire Knight. It was all because of him, then—she really had killed her own people just so people would stop following him.

But the stones in the sword only half glowed, and Maia frowned at her aunt, swallowing as bile splashed up her throat. "There's—more. Isn't there?"

Ismene gave her a condescending look, shaking her head, her chandelier-like earrings trembling, as if even they feared the queen. "Things your little mind would struggle to comprehend. Things the saints themselves demand, Maia."

True—the stones glowed.

"Those people needed to die," Ismene went on, not a dip or quaver in her conviction. "And that night prevented *countless* deaths. You can tell yourself that to soothe your conscience. Liann should never have been there; her death was her own fault." True, all true. Ismene sighed and shook her head again, observing Maia as she shook, gripping the dagger hard enough that her knuckles were bone white. "You had great promise, Maia, but your conscience corrupts you. If you'd been more like Yeven, with your power ... I would have made you my heir. But you're too much like my *sister*." Her voice twisted on that word.

Physically reining herself in, she waved a hand. "Go," she dismissed, already turning back to her sofa beside the fire. "Go to your room, or wherever else you scurry off to. I'll find a use for you, traitor or not."

Maia flashed cold. It started at the back of her neck, and then icy hands swept down her back, goosebumps covering her thighs. And then the chill was in her chest, squeezing her lungs until they were empty of air. She swore even her blood ran cold.

There'd be no torture, no sentencing, no execution—no end to this.

No end. Forever?

Maia couldn't catch a breath, but her tongue didn't feel quite so unwieldy in her mouth, and strength borne of anger, of pure white *refusal*, made her grip on the Dagger of Truths harder.

She looked down at the dagger, drawn to its fading glow, it's brutal hilt, and remembered the blade was more than just a truth teller, more than the magic in its stones. It was a honed edge, and an unbending knife, and a vicious, deadly point.

Maia was already a traitor, had already helped an enemy of the crown escape. All those fantasies rose up in her mind and took hold, and Maia wrapped them around her like the thickest, warmest cloak.

She swore there was a light touch on her shoulder, as if the saints were encouraging her.

Ismene was in the middle of returning to her seat on the sofa, sweeping the cream skirts of her cloudlike dress around her. Maia just *acted*. Her balance tipped forward, her boots gripping the carpet as she coiled her muscles and leapt. Air slid past, the world splitting to allow her through, her fae speed a blessing and a promise as years of training condensed into that one movement, that single act.

She couldn't breathe, but she didn't need to as she angled her dagger and threw her whole body into the blow. The blade cut effortlessly, piercing chiffon and fur and flesh and bone, as if it had been designed to kill a queen. Maia was screaming through gritted teeth, twenty-four years of hatred bleeding out as her momentum carried her onto the sofa, landing on top of her aunt and driving the blade deeper.

Ismene groaned, a deep sound of pain that made Maia grin nastily. Finally—finally she knew what it was like, had some tiny fucking inkling of how bad Etziel had hurt her. It wasn't enough—would never be enough—but it still felt fucking good.

With a ragged gasp of hope, Maia ripped the dagger out of her aunt's back, watching blood stain her pretty cream dress—and camouflaged against Maia's deep crimson skirts.

Numbness setting in, and wholly unwelcome, Maia stumbled off her aunt and away from the sofa, the dagger falling from her blood-slick hand. For a long moment she just panted, watching her aunt hiss and growl, twisting just enough on the settee to be able to glare at Maia. "I never knew," she panted, "you had a backbone."

Maia stepped forward, more than ready to grab the dagger from the floor and finish the job, but her wide eyes jumped to the slice in her aunt's dress, to the skin knitting together beneath it. Her blood went from ice to the impossible cold of the south, plummeting fast.

Ismene laughed, a garbled, horrible sound. "As if a knife could kill me."

Maia didn't give herself even a second to contemplate that. She wiped the blood from her hand on a chair as she stumbled past towards the door, dizzyingly grateful that these rooms were warded for protection against eavesdroppers, that none of the guards would have heard Ismene's cry.

"Where do you think you're going?" Ismene demanded, already sounding stronger. "Do you think you can hide? Etziel will find you."

Maia knew that, but unless she shut out the words, she'd never be able to function. She was already shaking, but she refused to let her blind panic show as she opened the door and quickly closed it behind herself. Her breathing shallow, she took step after step down the gilded hallway, past the Eversky's statue, and into the warren of corridors beyond it, not daring to look at any of the guards who'd ignored her silent pleas just minutes ago. When she was sure her footsteps didn't carry even to fae ears, Maia hitched up her skirt and ran, her shoes slapping the marble floors, her breathing a broken gasp.

She didn't stop to get her things from her room, not to find Naemi and beg her for help, not even as Lenka spotted her and called her name in concern. Maia didn't stop even as she reached the external side door and threw herself through it, onto a dark, tangled path that had been neglected by the Delakore gardeners for years. A path Maia had used as a kid, but most people forgot about. It was the tiniest glimmer of a chance, but she'd take even a mirage of hope right now.

Thorns scratched her arms as she shoved herself along the path, but they were nothing to the maelstrom of pain in Maia's chest, embedded in her soul. She didn't have a second to sort through the emotional wounds she'd been dealt, didn't have time for anything but dragging air into her lungs, pushing on through the thorns, and choking her sobs off before they crawled up her throat.

The path went on too long, her arms and the strip of midriff exposed by her dress savaged by the green spikes when she finally stumbled off the path at the end of it. It took her three attempts to unlatch the gate, the metal rattling in her quaking hands. They'd find her. She knew they would. Knew it was only a matter of time before these scratches were like feathers brushing skin compared to what Etziel would do.

But it didn't stop her sprinting down the tree-lined path, flinching at every rustling branch, every barge engine on the river at the bottom. She swore guards were following her, but the urgent footsteps crunching the layer of snow turned out to be her own, their laboured breaths her own, too.

The shaded path spat her out into the southside of Vassalaer, and Maia staggered across the street and into a busy intersection, praying she could disappear.

She couldn't go to the library, couldn't go anywhere Ismene would know to search. She'd send Etziel there first. But without the library, what options did Maia have? None. She had nowhere—and nobody who'd hide her, who'd keep her safe.

Maia choked on a sob, but she pushed on, racing past a florist peddling Eversky roses that flickered with magic bolts. No one clamoured around the woman, the palace quarter quiet as the sun spilled deep orange light on the cobbles. Maia was horrified to find the crowds were thin everywhere, even the markets mostly closed up at this time on a Sunday.

"Saints protect me," she rasped, a mad plea as she raced past the Eversky's Basilica, the lights in the terracotta spires turned low and candles snuffing out as night closed in. Maia ran until she spotted the sturdy crimson roof of the Vassal Theatre coming up ahead and her breath punched out of her lungs, the familiar sight making her shaky with relief. She couldn't go to the library, but the arts quarter was more a home to her than the palace had ever been, and a weight fell off her just to be here.

She wished suddenly that she'd made more friends here, introduced herself as Maia, just Maia, spoken more to the curators of the museums she'd visited monthly, made an effort to be more friendly to the sisters who guarded the vast stone archway rumoured to have been carved by the Hunchback Saint in memory of his fallen wife. If Maia had made *friends*, maybe she'd have had somewhere to go now, someone to turn to. The only person she'd ever spoken to was Dita and she had no idea where to find the woman other than at the Library of Vennh.

She'd thought she'd been safer that way, but all she'd done was isolate herself.

Her heart ached as she glimpsed the library's lapis towers and golden domes punching into the dark sapphire sky ahead of her, and the fragile organ broke clean in two as she veered right and away from it, skimming the riverside market where craftsmen and -women sold their wares during the day. Where it was a ghost town now.

The street lamps came on as she panted for air, her legs heavy and wobbly despite her training. Her dress was ragged where the thorns and thicket had torn at it, the tang of copper on her tongue from the blood running down her arms, and she fought a wince as cold bit at every exposed slice of skin as if in warning.

She didn't realise where she was running, didn't know the library had put the thought in her head, until she glimpsed the statues of Sorvauw Bridge, luminous against the deep red sky.

Yes, she agreed with whatever instinctive part of her had been running towards that little house on the river, towards the Sapphire Knight's home. He was the crown's enemy, *her* enemy, but his home might be the only place Maia would be safe. As long as he never realised she was anything more than Maia, the librarian.

She'd just made it to the covered stage beside the bridge when sharp metal bit into her arm, and a deep cry ripped up her throat, sending her stumbling into the side of a covered food stall.

A dart was embedded in her arm, blood and greenish fluid leaking from its tip. She'd ... been shot. She'd been *shot*.

"Shit," Maia hissed, her throat closing up as Hope started to die a rapid death. Her hand shaking fiercely, she ripped the dart out and kept running, ignoring the sting. Poison— she'd been poisoned. He was close.

"Please," she begged the saints, as if they'd listen. "*Please.*"

"Where are you running to, Maia?" Etziel called from behind her, his voice gloating.

She'd been an idiot to stay on this side of the river; she should have crossed the Luvasa immediately, and lost him among the parliamentary buildings on the other side of the city.

"No," she whispered, not an answer to his question, but an answer for herself. *No*, she would not be taken, dragged back to the palace, and tortured. *No*, she would not live the rest of her life as a thing to be used by her aunt whenever she wanted someone controlled or killed.

No.

That was not who Maia was, not who she wanted to be. Not anymore.

She refused to go back. She'd rather throw herself into the river. But instead she sprinted onto the smooth stones of the bridge, and prayed to the saints that she reached that house by the river, even as she knew it was hopeless and she was already caught.

CHAPTER EIGHTEEN

The statues and columns of Sorvauw Bridge wavered and tilted in Maia's vision, the tall stone buildings on the riverside curving in around her like malevolent figures. She didn't dare look at the faces of the stone saints as she ran, keeping her eyes fixed straight ahead even as the world tipped and twisted around her.

"You can't run, Maia," Etziel taunted, his voice chillingly calm as she wavered and bumped into the column where the Wolven Lord's face should have been, long chipped away to anonymity. "The fevreweed in your system is already at work, shutting down your senses."

Maia shook her head, frantically trying to clear it and only making the dizziness worse. Amber lights from windows formed streaks like shooting stars as she staggered, thick viscous poison dripping down her shoulder. Blood trailed down her arms too, slicking her hands; she left a smear on the forsaken saint's column as she dragged in a tight, rasping breath and pushed on, swaying three more steps down the bridge.

She *had* to keep going. Etziel wanted her dizzy and

unconscious for a reason, and every possibility made her bones shake, her teeth rattling in her ears. She'd been a child when he last made her scream in agony. How much worse would it be now she was fully grown?

Get across the bridge, she told herself desperately. *You just have to get across the bridge.*

But the bridge was an insurmountable distance to cross, especially as numbness started to spread down her legs and her knees buckled as a gust of wind hit like a battering ram. She caught herself on the column of the Graceless Swan, cold stone biting into her palms, and she left another smear on the pale column, like a trail of crumbs. The saint of mistakes and redemption watched impassively as Maia used the smooth, weatherworn marble of her column to launch herself a few more steps down the bridge.

Wind from the river tore at her hair, her skirts, and Maia's next breath was horribly laboured. She wasn't going to make it. Etziel was going to get bored; he was going to grab a fistful of her hair and haul her back up to the palace again.

"But by all means," he went on, a laugh twining through his pleasant voice a few meters behind, "try to run, princess. It makes my night more interesting."

Maia gritted her teeth and fought against the cold slush that moved through her bloodstream, fear making her shake all over. How long did she have before her legs failed completely? How long until Etziel was upon her? Her breath sawed out of her lungs, her boots scuffing the stone as clumsy legs carried her towards the Hunchback Saint's statue. Each saint was a goal, a desperate marker on her path to safety. She didn't care that they were stone, that they couldn't really encourage her or witness what was about to happen. They were her stoic companions, and the thought of having the saints on side gave her strength.

She wasn't going to make it to the end of the bridge, but that didn't stop her trying.

She managed seven more faltering steps, clinging to the wall, only able to make that little progress because Etziel was playing with her, *taunting* her with the barest hope that she'd escape. When she'd plunged the Dagger of Truths into her aunt's back, she'd thought that was it, the nightmare finally ended, one way or another. Either she'd be free or she'd be dead. But no, Ismene would keep her alive, the nightmare never ending. For the rest of her pitiful existence. Forever.

Maia wouldn't go back to it. She refused to.

She *had* to make it across the bridge, had to make it to the terrace house by the river. It was the only place she might be safe. Even that wasn't guaranteed, but it was all she had, and she clung to it.

Maia took another step, her heart clamouring up her throat, but her foot gave out and she crumpled to the rough stone, pain exploding through her kneecap and shoulder as they hit the unforgiving bridge and skin scraped raw. Her head lolled, and for a reckless moment, she just laid there, dazed and breathless and scared beyond belief. There was only the cold and the pain spiking through her chest with every rise and fall, agony drumming through her shoulder, and the saints as silent witness. There was nothing else on this wind-tossed bridge in that endless moment after she fell. She wanted to curl up and cry, but if she did that, her life was forfeit. She had to scrape her agonised body off the floor, and keep running.

"Got you," Etziel said, a smile in his voice as his boot slammed into Maia's ribs. No warning, no hint of it coming —just blinding pain mauling her middle, her throat hoarse as a scream forced its way out.

Her breaths became shards of jagged air that hurt to inhale, and tears veiled her vision in a blinding sheet as she curled around herself, hands shaking, death so close she could feel the wolves breathing down her neck, and the abyss's heat blistering her skin.

Was this how she would die? On a bridge she'd crossed so many times she'd lost count, in a city she'd loved for as long as she could remember?

But it wasn't death that Etziel offered. He would drag her back to servitude and fear, shove her into that life and watch her choke on it.

She wouldn't go back.

She *wouldn't*.

Power burned through her chest, or maybe it was blind, stupid stubbornness that dug its heels in. Whatever it was, it strengthened Maia as she gritted her teeth and flattened her palms against the rough stone of the bridge, a brush of soft velvet under her fingers—the petal that had fallen from her bodice. She left it there on the bridge; it had given her little luck so far, why should it help her now?

Little stones dug into her hands as she pushed back, but she ignored every gasp of pain. Her lungs had to be scratched raw, her body battered, and pain made everything harder, an uphill battle it was almost impossible to win. Almost.

"I'm not dying here, not at your hand," Maia snarled, panting for breath, his scent of apples and blood clinging to her throat. But it was enough, a vow to the saints watching, a message and a warning to whoever dared to bet against her. "I'm not dying here."

Etziel laughed, crouching beside her as Maia heaved herself into a sitting position, her back thumping against the bridge's stone wall. She panted and blinked, her surroundings spinning like a merry-go-round, lamplight and starlight blurring together into one bright magic-like streak.

"Then where would you rather die?" he asked, amusement shining through his courtly veneer. "I'm amenable to suggestions. Let the saints observe my graciousness and hospitality."

Maia sucked in a breath and steeled her nerves, braced for the pain she knew would break her in two. "Let the saints observe *this*," she hissed, and snapped her forehead into his nose, hot blood splashing across her face. Holy *fuck*, that hurt. She gritted her teeth as the world crashed in a painful blur, but Etziel fell back with a grunt, grabbing his face as blood spurted. She'd accomplished that, at least. Warmth bloomed on her shoulder, and Maia took it as a saint urging her to get up.

She dug her fingernails into the wall behind her and hauled herself to her feet, stumbling away as fast as her bruised body would allow.

Slow, too slow, but she didn't stop her faltering run, grateful for the wind pushing at her heels, making her faster.

Five feet to the end of the bridge, now.

Four feet. She could see the house—Azrail's house.

Three feet. She didn't dare breathe, her whole body buzzing with anticipation and pain.

"You can't get away, Maia," Etziel said, his voice thick with blood. "There's nowhere you can hide that I won't find you."

"Wanna bet?" Maia spat weakly, pressing a hand to her ribs as agony blared through the place he'd kicked her at her jerky, rushed movements.

Two feet. The stone steps down to the riverside were within view.

One foot. *Please—please*.

Maia couldn't breathe as she grabbed at the wall and stumbled towards the steps, bits of mortar embedding under her fingernails. But with her foot on the top step she realised that reaching the end of the bridge was only the first obstacle. Now, she had to get down the tall, narrow staircase to the riverside on numb, uncooperative legs.

But it turned out getting to the bottom was easy as tripping over her numb feet. A breathless scream tore from her lips as her body slid out from beneath her, and she could do nothing to stop herself tumbling down the river-slick steps. Her screams became whimpers as hard, stone edges slammed mercilessly into her body, cutting and breaking her open until there was no part of her that wasn't in agony, until she tasted her own blood.

She saw nothing beyond a speeding blur, the fall too fast to process, and she landed in a bruised, bloody heap at the bottom, stunned into stillness. For an endless minute, Maia just stared at the starlit sky overhead as the heavens opened and drops of rain fell onto her body, every part of her screaming with pain. Her mind screamed, too, a deafening refusal to go back to the palace, to her aunt, to that life of never saying no. The raindrops were cool and soothing, the Eversky's comfort making Maia's eyes slide shut.

But that glade inside her soul stretched out a branch, beseeching her, a tiny, precious leaf unfurling on its edge. Hope—she wasn't caught yet. Battered and broken and certainly on the edge of capture. But she wasn't caught *yet*.

Maia dragged her eyelids apart with a groan of pain. Etziel was going to catch her. She only had to make it five houses down this riverside path, she reminded herself. *Just five houses, you can do that.*

If she sat up, she'd be able to see the house she'd watched the Sapphire Knight disappear into. She was close—so close to almost-safety.

The glade rattled its branches within her, an urgent encouragement, and Maia pushed onto her elbows with a garbled scream. The terrace houses and the dark river went black as she fought her way to her knees, nearly tipping back to the floor, but she threw out a hand automatically to catch herself on the wall to her left, her palms not the only thing leaving bloody streaks anymore. If she'd fallen even a metre more to her right ... the Luvasa would have swallowed her.

But better the Luvasa than the twisted man stalking her, laughing softly as he reached the top of the stairs and beheld what a broken mess she'd become.

No more resting, she breathed to herself, and swore the warm hand on her shoulder pushed at her. *Time to get up now.*

Getting to her feet was an agony, the world cutting out to blackness again, but she gritted her teeth and refused to surrender to unconsciousness. She'd never thought it was possible to be in this much pain and still be alive, but the torment only increased, growing until she couldn't see anything but blurs when the blackness receded.

But Etziel's soft laugh had her moving, sheer instinct propelling her into a shambling walk down the row of houses. With shaking, bloody hands, she held onto the steel railings that fenced in their neat, boxy gardens, but Maia didn't make out any of their contents as she put one aching leg in front of the other. She counted each gate she passed, screaming through clenched teeth with every step, making painstaking progress.

Behind, she could hear Etziel skipping slowly down the steps after her. He didn't realise she had an end destination yet; he thought she was only trying to run from him. Maia prayed to the saints that he didn't figure it out, that he didn't know who lived here as she passed another gate.

One more house, and she was there. One more.

Her ankle had twisted in the fall, and pain arrowed through her leg with every halting step she took. Maia tried to ignore that the rest of her body was every bit as ruined, warm blood running down the side of her face, a startling contrast to the cool rain.

One more house, and you're safe. Just one more.

The world went black again as pain shot up her leg, but her hand found the cold latch of the next gate, and her bottom lip wobbled. She prayed she'd counted correctly as she fumbled the gate open and dragged herself up the path, hauling up whatever reserves she had left for those even steps. Only the glade in her soul, unfurling branches of encouragement with every step she took, kept her moving. Power reached through her insides like a warm hug, keeping her mercifully upright as she raised a fist and slammed it into the door. Her arm was so heavy that it fell to her side on the third knock, and her hand left a smear of blood on the cobalt door.

"Please," she breathed, her voice shaky, dizziness of the fevreweed catching up to her as she slumped against the door, the cold wood a blessed relief. "Please…"

Etziel was closer now, his footsteps confident and unhurried. "No one's going to help you there, Maia. These houses all belong to northsiders."

She said nothing, leaning her forehead against the cool, soothing wood of the door, her eyes sliding shut as rain soaked her hair, making her dress heavy and cold.

Please…

She fell forward as the door swung away, tasting blood on her lips as she cried out. Her eyes flew open on instinct as she hurtled towards the ground—and was caught in arms that were an agony to her open wounds.

Behind her, Etziel swore, footsteps moving swiftly away. She sobbed, her breathing shattered to sharp, painful shards as she blinked dizzily at a face she recognised. So handsome it hurt, his eyes the purest, deepest blue.

"I had nowhere else to go," she slurred, and passed out in Azrail's arms.

Thank you for picking up my newest series - I hope you loved Heir of Ruin! There is much, *much* more in store for Maia, starting with book two Heart of Thorns, where she grows closer to her harem and the beastkind mystery deepens. It releases in June 2021.

Leigh

P.s. sorry for the sliiiightly evil cliffhanger.

THANK YOU FOR READING!

I hope you enjoyed Heir of Ruin!

Need the next book ASAP? Let me know – the more demand for a series, the more likely I am to bump the next book to the top of my list! To stay updated with what I'm working on next, come join me in my Paranormal Den on Facebook, or sign up to my fortnightly newsletter! (Links on the next pages, so keep reading, loves.)

If this is your first Leigh Kelsey book, I have lots more books for you to sink your teeth into, and four completed series. I've got vampires, wolves, dragons, angels, and demons - and of course plenty of growly alpha males with tragic backstories.

※

Reviews make the world go 'round - or at least they do in my world. If you loved this book and you can spare a minute, please leave a review on Amazon or wherever else you like to review. Even the smallest, one-line review has an impact, and helps me reach new readers like you awesome people.

Thank you to everyone who's already reviewed. Your words mean I can keep writing the books you love!

LEIGH KELSEY
REVERSE HAREM ROMANCE AUTHOR

JOIN MY READER GROUP!

To get news about upcoming releases before anywhere else, and early access to my books, come join my reader group over on Facebook!

THREE FREEBIES FOR YOU

Fancy some freebies? I'll send you three when you join my newsletter! I promise never to spam you, and I rarely send more frequently than once a fortnight so you won't be overloaded with emails.

Join here: https://madmimi.com/signups/03d55060b9ad4e619393482b30bc1138/join

COMPLETE RH WOLF SHIFTER SERIES!

Having every male werewolf in the area lining up to claim you might sound like a good thing, but belonging to a wolf is Lyra's worst nightmare. Too bad she's about to belong to three.

READ FREE IN KINDLE UNLIMITED

COMPLETE RH ANGEL/DEMON FANTASY SERIES!

Betrayed by heaven, protected by hell. The devil and his hellhounds will do anything to keep their angel safe.

READ FREE IN KINDLE UNLIMITED

COMPLETE RH DRAGON SHIFTER
SERIES!

They cuffed her.
Branded her.
Locked her up, and threw away the key.
But Trouble won't let these a*holes break her.

READ FREE IN KINDLE UNLIMITED

COMPLETE RH VAMPIRE SERIES!

A blood-drenched legacy. Three devoted lovers. An ancient evil rising.

Elara will be lucky to survive her new life as a vampire...

READ FREE IN KINDLE UNLIMITED

ABOUT THE AUTHOR

Leigh Kelsey is the author of sweet and steamy books for anyone with a soft spot for steely women and the tortured men who love them. No matter what stories she's writing – vampires or shifters or rebels – they all share a common thread of romance, heart, and action. She is the author of the Lili Kazana series, the Vampire Game series, the Moonlight Inn series, and the Second Breath Academy series. Leigh also writes new adult and young adult books under the name Saruuh Kelsey.

FIND THESE OTHER BOOKS BY LEIGH KELSEY!

All solo books free on Kindle Unlimited

Call of Magic (99c Paranormal, Urban Fantasy, and Fantasy stories)

Captured and Captivated (Alien and Sci-Fi Romance)
Happily Furever After (Animal Charity Anthology)
Kiss of Magic (PNR w/ Curvy Women)
Love Bites (Paranormal Vampire Romance)

Stand Alone Stories
Sinful Beauty (RH Demon Romance Stand-Alone)

Fae of the Saintlands series
Heir of Ruin
Heart of Thorns

Blacktower Prison for Supernaturals series
(complete series)
Prison of Embers
Tower of Sparks
Fortress of Flame
Refuge of Firelight

Lili Kazana series
(complete series)
Complete Series Box Set (w/ exclusive epilogue!)
Cast From Heaven

Crowned By Hell

Called By Gods

Vampire Game series
(complete series)
Complete Series Box Set
Vampire Game
Vampire Touch
Vampire Legacy

Moonlight Inn series
(complete series)
Complete Series Box Set (w/ exclusive epilogue!)
Mated
Empowered
Unlimited
Ascended
Unleashed
Victorious

Dead Space Universe
Dead Space (RH Sci-Fi Stand-Alone)

Second Breath Academy series
How To Raise The Dead
How To Kill A Ghost